A MAGNOLIA FRIENDSHIP

THE RED STILETTO BOOK CLUB SERIES

ANNE-MARIE MEYER

SHARI

The package sitting on my dresser was hard to ignore. It was as if a giant dragon had perched itself there and was staring at me, daring me to pick it up. It looked innocent enough. The light-brown paper with the black lettering shouldn't be as intimidating as it felt. But in its plain appearance, it mocked me. I knew exactly what it held inside.

My divorce papers.

I sighed as I finished buttoning up my shirt and pulled my hair out of the ponytail it had been in all day. My soft brown hair swished at my shoulders. In an effort to reinvent myself, I'd allowed Clementine to convince me to visit Mia at Clip and Snip, the local stylist here in Magnolia.

She'd done a fabulous job trimming the dead and fraying ends that I'd allowed to accumulate while I was going through the drama with Craig. Getting it cut felt symbolic for what I'd done when I walked out on Craig the night I discovered exactly why our marriage was failing.

When I'd discovered the other woman.

Freeing myself from the damage he caused helped me see the kind of person I wanted to be, even though I wasn't that person yet. Going from an intact family to a broken one was never going to be simple—I knew that— but I just hadn't anticipated how soul-crushing it would be.

Seeing Bella tear up and Tag close down when I told them that their dad was moving out and living across the bridge was enough for me to fear that I'd made the wrong choice. It was almost enough for me to drag Craig's sorry butt back here and attempt to make it work.

But then the memory of living under the same roof as my cheating husband washed over me, and I pushed those thoughts from my mind. Instead of getting back together, I was going to figure out how to make my new normal work for my family.

It wasn't ideal. But I was going to make sure that my children never wanted for anything. They were my world, and I was going to make sure that they knew that. Every day.

After slipping on my sandals, I opened my door and made my way out to the kitchen. The sound of Jake and Clementine's laughter mixed with Bella's was like music to my ears. Tonight was a book club meeting, and Jake had offered to watch the kids so that Clementine and I could have a night out.

It'd been three months since he'd moved back home. Once I'd decided to leave Craig and Jake had decided that he couldn't live without Clementine, we'd spent most of the summer camping and fishing with the kids. It had been nice having them around. They helped me feel less lonely and isolated. They forced me out even if I didn't want to go.

Clementine was consumed with getting her dance studio together, and Jake was learning the ropes of the hardware store he was going to take over. I was happy that they both had found a place to put down roots and a person to love. They were happy, and if I were completely honest, I was jealous of that happiness.

Was I ever going to feel that way again?

"Uh oh." Jake's teasing smile popped up in front of me. I blinked a few times as I brought my thoughts back to the present.

"What?" I asked as I whacked his arm.

Jake pulled back, pinching his lips and shaking his head. "Nothing. Nothing," he repeated.

I shot him a dirty look as I crossed the kitchen and pulled open the fridge to grab out a bottle of orange juice. I was in the middle of pouring when he made his way over to me. Just as I set my glass down, his arm wrapped around my shoulders, and suddenly, I was being pulled into a side-crushing hug.

I wiggled, but when I realized there was no way I was

going to be able to escape his embrace, I relaxed and turned to glare at him. "Can I help you?" I asked. Even though I enjoyed having him around, I didn't enjoy the fact that, every so often, he looked at me as if to ask "Everything okay?"

It only made me realize that, perhaps, I wasn't okay. And then all of my doubt, all of my worry, would creep up, causing butterflies to attack my stomach and take over my nerves.

It was as if he were sawing at the very thin thread that was holding my life together. Eventually I was going to snap—and I couldn't afford to snap.

Not right now.

So I jabbed him the ribs, causing him to flinch and pull back. I took his moment of weakness as my signal to move and spun away. Just as I stopped myself on the counter perpendicular to him, Clementine let out a cheer. I glanced over at her to see her grinning in my direction.

"Perfect spin-out," she said, motioning toward me.

I scoffed as I glanced around, but my cheeks heated from her praise. There was no hiding the fact that I had two left feet when it came to anything dancing related. So the fact that Clementine gave me a compliment—even if I doubted her words—made me feel embarrassed.

As if she sensed my unease, Clementine cleared her throat and smiled over at Jake. "Well, we should get going," she said as she made her way over and linked arms with me. She peeked over at me, and I nodded.

"Yeah, we don't want to be late." I eyed my brother. "Think you can handle this?"

Jake laughed as he made his way over to Bella and picked her up, slinging her over his shoulder. She squealed with excitement as her hand moved to grip the back of his shirt. "I think we'll be fine." He bumped his shoulder, causing Bella to bounce.

Her giggle turned into a shrill, and I attempted to shush her, but that was like trying to stop a raging river with a stick. He was riling her up, and I knew if I was going to enjoy my evening without worrying about my children, I needed to leave.

With my stilettos in hand, I followed Clementine as she led the way to the back door. Before I stepped outside, I turned to meet Jake's gaze. "Do something with the monster," I mouthed as I nodded toward Tag's room.

I thought things with Tag were hard when Craig was around, but I had been kidding myself. They were ten times worse now that he was no longer here. I didn't know if Tag felt as if his father's absence meant he didn't need to respect me or if I'd failed him completely as his mother—but things were bad.

He was refusing to speak to me, and most of the time I couldn't get him out of his room. Hopefully with me gone, his beloved uncle Jake would be able to talk some sense into the kid. And maybe convince him to take a shower. The room was beginning to smell like a hazard area—I was going to have to condemn it any day now.

Jake gave me a quick nod. I felt a tad relieved and

hopeful that he was going to get further than I'd been able to. I turned and headed out to Clementine's car. We piled in and took off toward the inn.

The group was smaller today. Besides me, Clementine, Maggie, and Victoria, the only other person who joined us was Fiona. She was new to the island and younger. I tried to talk to her a few times, but I ended up feeling ancient. I wouldn't mind being her friend—if I didn't feel as if I could somehow be her mother.

Which, when I broke it down, was impossible. I would have to have been fifteen when I gave birth, but still. It was a possibility. A weird and awkward possibility that I preferred not to think about.

With our heels on, we sat around Maggie's kitchen island while we drank margaritas and ate chips that Clementine had picked up from the local Mexican restaurant. The books we'd brought were stacked on the counter next to us, but it seemed as if no one was really interested in talking about them.

Which, if I were honest with myself, I was completely on board with. A night out with the girls was exactly what I needed.

"How's the studio going?" Maggie asked as she glanced over at Clementine, who was mid-bite.

She quickly chewed and took a sip of her drink before she responded. "Good. Just finishing up some final touches. We should be ready to open middle of next month."

We all nodded, and I made a mental note to ask her

about classes for Bella. But before anyone could speak, Clementine cleared her throat and her cheeks hinted pink as she peered around at us.

I furrowed my brow, fully understanding what this look meant. Clementine was about to do something devious.

"Actually, I wanted to talk to you ladies about a class I'm thinking about bringing to the studio."

I grabbed a chip and dipped it into the salsa. "Spill it, chica," I said.

Everyone had their gaze focused on Clementine as she took in a deep breath and then parted her lips.

"I'm thinking about getting Archer to install some poles in the back of the studio and starting a pole dancing class."

Just as the last three words left her lips, I inhaled, causing a bit of chip to fly to the back of my throat and lodge itself there. I started hawking and pounding my chest. From the corner of my eye, I saw Maggie stand and grab a bottle of water from the fridge. When I finally dislodged it, my eyes were watering and my throat felt raw.

I glanced around to see that everyone was staring at me. I offered them a weak smile through my watering eyes. They chuckled and turned back to focus on Clementine.

"Pole dancing is amazing for your core," Clementine continued. "I just want to know if anyone would be interested before I have them installed." She glanced around to all of us. "What do you think?"

I widened my eyes as I watched Maggie and Fiona nod with fervent glee. Victoria just sat there with her arms folded and her nose wrinkled as if she'd just smelled something bad. Not wanting to be in the Victoria camp, I smiled and nodded along with the other two. Even though when it came down to it, I doubted I could get my post-babies hips up any pole.

"Sounds fun," I said as I offered Clementine an encouraging smile. Her own smile deepened, and I could tell that my friend was excited about this. And even though I didn't want to, if taking a class would help her out, I was willing to do it.

Clementine got a far-off look in her eyes as she leaned back in her chair and folded her arms. "It's going to be epic."

We all laughed, and the conversation drifted away into silence. I grabbed another chip just as Fiona perked up.

"Well, since we aren't going to be talking about the book, how about we do something else?" She tapped her fingers on the countertop in front of her.

"Something else? Why would we do something else?" Victoria asked.

I could hear the annoyance in her voice as she shifted on her seat. Growing up with her had taught me a lot about her personality. She liked rules. She liked order. So the idea that we were going to throw that all out the window had to be bothering her.

And it made me wonder why she was even here. After all, with her reelection just around the corner, I would have figured she would be swamped with campaigning and focusing on making her second run as Magnolia's mayor a success. She had never been the type to value a friendship over a goal.

At least, that was how she'd treated me when she ditched me in high school. We'd been friends once, but not anymore.

We were anything but.

"What do you have in mind?" I asked as I turned to Fiona, not being shy in ignoring Victoria's comment. Fiona had a glint in her eye that made me feel nervous and excited at the same time. Right now, I had more in common with her in the relationship department than I did with pretty much anyone else in the room.

Victoria didn't count, and Maggie and Clementine had both found their lifelong partners. With the package looming over me at home, I was on my way to being single-Shari. And I didn't know what that meant or how I was supposed to act. At least with Fiona around, we could both be single moms together.

There was solidarity in finding someone in the same situation as me.

"There's a new club opening up across the bridge," she said, perking up from my question.

I nearly choked, again, on the chip I'd just finished chewing. A club? Was she serious? I may have gotten ahead of myself thinking we could have anything in common.

"A club?" Clementine asked as if she could read my mind.

Fiona nodded. "I hear it's super fun." She dropped back against the back of her chair. "Blake just got over a stomach bug, and I'm in need of a break just to prove to myself that I'm a woman and not a throw-up rag."

I stared at her. It was as if she was speaking to me. That was exactly how I felt. How was I going to shift from *mom* to *woman* when I wasn't even sure how to be *woman*? I couldn't help but think that, perhaps, Fiona held the key to that door, and I was standing in front of it, waiting for it to open.

"I don't know…" Maggie said.

"I'm for it." The words were out of my lips before I could stop myself. I instantly regretted them when suddenly everyone was staring at me—they looked a bit too surprised if I were honest. It was as if no one thought that going to a club might be something I could enjoy. "What?" I asked, shrugging off their looks with completely fabricated confidence.

"Nothing," Clementine said as a smile emerged on her lips that was little too gleeful. It was as if I'd surprised her —but in a good way.

"Great! Shari's on board. Who else? Victoria?" Fiona asked.

Victoria looked at each of us and then sighed. "Fine. I can't believe that we are going to turn into *that* kind of book club." She flicked her red hair over her shoulder and sighed. "But I don't want to go home tonight, so let's do this."

Fiona cheered, clapping her hands as she motioned toward Maggie and Clementine. "How about it, ladies? Up for some partying?" Fiona bent her arms and began shifting her shoulders to a nonexistent beat.

Clementine laughed and stood. "If there's dancing, I'm there. Let me call Jake and tell him where we are going."

Maggie looked a little pale, but she eventually gave a small nod as she moved to stand. I stood up as well and helped Maggie clear the table. Once the garbage was thrown away and the chip crumbs were wiped down, we gathered on the porch as we waited for the rideshare car to come pick us up.

The air around us was filled with laughter as we listened to Maggie recount a situation where a patron got so drunk, they passed out on the stairs. Her imitation of Archer cursing and sweating as he tried to carry the man up the stairs was hysterical.

It wasn't until we were in the car and on the way across the bridge that panic set in. This was not me. At all. I was never a partier even when I was a rebel teenager, and the fact that I was attempting to do this at my age made me feel like a foreigner in my own body.

As much as I wanted to actually be as brave as I was attempting to be, I knew the truth. I wasn't the kind of woman who partied. I wasn't the kind of woman who stayed out until all hours of the night surrounded by men.

I wasn't the kind of woman who drank and danced with her friends.

And even though I knew I wasn't that kind of woman, I couldn't help but wonder what it was like. I couldn't help but wonder, what if I was?

And that kind of thinking made me feel frightened, sure, but mostly it made me feel...free.

2

VICTORIA

This was ridiculous. How had I let Fiona and the rest of the girls talk me into this? They looked so at ease with each other, laughing and dancing like they'd been bosom buddies since kindergarten. Every time I attempted to enter the conversation, I ended up coming across as awkward and, at times, way too loud—even for my own ears.

My entire body burned with embarrassment as the women I'd come with attempted to appease my quirks. They smiled and nodded as if I hadn't just embarrassed myself, but I knew better. I made them uncomfortable— I'd been alive long enough to know what their expressions meant even if they were trying to pretend my being here didn't bother them. I was the struggling idiot who was attempting to fit in where I didn't belong.

Sawyer had insisted that I attempt to befriend the

locals. He said that it would help with my image in the town. That if I wanted even a chance at reelection, I was going to have to start building a foundation with the residents here.

Apparently giving my whole life to the town I'd grown up in wasn't enough. I needed to prove to Magnolia that I was the loving, carefree mayor they wanted.

I couldn't hide behind my name anymore.

If I wanted the mayoral seat—I was going to have to prove to my constituents that I deserved it. And being part of the Red Stiletto Book Club was step one in my quest to redefine who Victoria Holt was.

If only I could belong effortlessly like Maggie did—despite her being here for only a few months. She seemed as if she'd been in Magnolia her whole life. While I felt as if I were a stranger staring in through the front window.

I really wasn't part of the book club group, and standing in a sweaty, smelly, strobing club wasn't where I belonged either. In fact, if one more guy leered at me or stepped on my foot, I was going to throw a fit and flip him on his back. I didn't take all of those jujitsu classes for nothing.

Joao, my trainer, would be so proud.

"Here you go," the bartender said as he placed a wine cooler onto the bar.

I straightened and turned to grab the ice-cold bottle. The cool temperature shocked my fingertips and helped ground me in the present. I'd had enough internal dialogue this evening to last me a lifetime.

"Thanks," I mumbled. When I glanced up, I saw the bright blue eyes of the bartender, and for a moment, I allowed my gaze to roam over his features. His dirty-blond hair was styled in a way that gave the impression he didn't care—when it was obvious he did.

His jaw was chiseled, and he had the right amount of stubble to make him look professionally unkempt. I couldn't help the smile that emerged as I pulled my drink closer to me. If I was going to be in this godforsaken place, I might as well have some fun. And this guy looked like fun.

"Brett." Maggie's voice startled me, and I turned to see her walk up to us with a wide smile. She must have had a lot to drink because she was exceptionally giggly at the moment.

I glanced back to who I could only assume was Brett as he leaned forward over the counter. "Hey, Maggie."

So his name was Brett. Good to know. He definitely didn't live in Magnolia, that I was sure of. It was my job to catalogue every resident, which was more of a curse than a blessing. I was acutely aware of the lack of dating material that existed in my hometown.

"I didn't know you worked here," Maggie said as she leaned both elbows on the counter.

"Do you know each other?" I asked as I flicked my pointer finger between the two of them.

Maggie nodded as she swatted Brett's arm. He smiled but raised his eyebrows at the same time. "Brett is the new chef at Magnolia. He's phenomenal. A real-life hero.

My life saver," Maggie said before she erupted into giggles.

Brett chuckled as he glanced over at me. "She may be overselling me a tad," he said. He'd lowered his voice, and it had a sort of sexy drawl to it that caused me to lean in closer to him. It'd been a while since a man intrigued me, and color me intrigued.

Maggie shook her head. "I'm not lying. You need to come to the inn, Victoria, and have some of his food." She pressed her fingertips to her lips and kissed them like an Italian chef.

Brett chuckled, and I couldn't help my gaze as it traveled back to him. He seemed so relaxed and at ease that, for a moment, I felt jealous of this stranger. I wanted to be relaxed and at ease. But that thought floated away as reality came crashing down around me.

I was Victoria Holt. Daughter of Senator Holt and the mayor of Magnolia. There was nothing fun or relaxing about my life or my job. It was a joke that I'd even allowed myself to entertain that thought.

So I picked up my wine cooler and held it up to Brett. "It was nice to meet you."

He nodded as he grabbed a fresh glass and began to fill it with ice for the twenty-something girl who was giggling a little too loud as her gaze raked over Brett.

"Maybe I'll see you at the inn?" he called after me.

I shrugged and turned, cursing the butterflies that took flight inside of my stomach. What was I doing? Was I serious? This was election year—it wasn't the time to have butterflies for anything but winning.

If I even attempted to walk down a path that intrigued me—namely Brett—I was going to lose the election. And Holts don't lose. We dominate. Period.

I shook my head, and by the time I got over to where Clementine, Fiona, and Shari were, my mind had cleared for the most part. I made sure to situate myself so that my back was to the bar.

Different songs started up and I began to feel old. I hadn't heard most of the ones that got the club goers to their feet. Instead, I leaned against the table for support as I sipped my drink.

We'd been idiots to think that wearing our stilettos would be fun. We just looked like weird friends who insisted on matching—and that was when we weren't stumbling over our feet as we tried to walk. Thankfully, I had some experience living in heels. My job required business formal every day. But Shari and Clementine were struggling, and it was almost comical to watch them walk like newborns across the club.

I'd had enough of standing around, not dancing, and not really being able to talk. Exhaustion took over. I leaned into Maggie, who'd taken a break from dancing to come back to the table for a drink of water.

"I'm going to split," I said as I shouldered my purse. I was ready to go home, take a bath, and crawl into bed.

Since Mom and Dad were back at the family house, I

was also ready to get their lecture about the mayor staying out all hours over with so I could finally fall asleep.

Tomorrow was a busy day of campaigning, and with Dad home to focus on my reelection, there was going to be no rest for the wicked.

It was going to be full speed until election day.

Maggie furrowed her brow. "Are you sure? I mean, you can stay. It won't be the same without you."

I tossed my bottle in a nearby trash can as I shook my head. "Nah, I'm ready to go." I turned and headed through the club and out the front doors before she had the chance to say anything else. The thrumming of the bass could be heard outside as the doors slowly closed behind me. Once they were shut and the noise dulled, I finally felt like I could hear, despite the ringing in my ears.

Taking in a deep breath, I tipped my head back and closed my eyes. The air was cleaner out here, and the trill of bugs helped sooth my ragged nerves. I was a little tipsy from the alcohol, but it wasn't anything I couldn't handle. I'd spent countless nights at evening parties, drinking with some of the political elites.

There wasn't much that could shake me, and I knew my limits. I never let myself get too tipsy. My job required poise and elegance no matter the circumstance.

The sound of a car pulling up drew my attention, and relief flooded over me when I saw that it was a cab. Talk about fortuitous timing. I waited outside for the door to open, and a moment later, I was met with two very familiar brown eyes and a mess of curly brown hair.

My jaw dropped as I flung my arms around my baby brother and pulled him into a hug. "Danny!" I exclaimed.

He was tense at first, but then a moment later, he laughed as he squeezed me like he'd always done in the past. "Tori?" he asked as he pulled back to stare at me. I slugged his shoulder, and he dropped his arms to pull away from me. "Geez," he said, "I see you're still just as violent as I remember."

I narrowed my eyes at him but couldn't dispel the smile that played on my lips. "I didn't know you were coming home." After graduation from law school. Daniel took off to Greece without so much as a goodbye or a look back. The last I heard—besides the occasional tag in a social media post—Mom was lamenting that she once had a son, but not anymore.

While I was tied down to this town, Danny got to be free. As much as I loved my baby brother, I couldn't help but feel as if he lived the life I'd always wanted. He got to fly away from the nest with no responsibilities or commitments to hold him down.

His tanned skin and casual attire was proof of his freedom. He wasn't beholden to the Holt-family appearance. He could be whomever he wanted to be.

I wasn't sure who I wanted to be besides Victoria, mayor of Magnolia. Or how to be anything else but that.

Daniel was still rubbing his arm as he studied me. "I didn't want Mom to make a big deal about it." He leaned forward. "Can you keep it hush-hush until I make my way back?"

I sighed as I stared at him. Telling our parents that he was home would help take the heat off of me—but he was my kid brother, and even though he was only three years from thirty, I could respect his wishes for a few days. Reality was an inevitable foe, and at some point, he would have to face it. Might as well let him push it off.

"I'm telling them on Sunday if you're not back yet," I said as I sidestepped him and leaned into the open cab. "Magnolia?" The driver nodded, and I straightened to say goodbye to Daniel.

He glowered at me with his arms folded and a look in his eyes that I knew was his attempt to intimidate me, but it just made him look adorable. Sort of like the kid who I'd caught in my room, stealing my makeup because he wanted to be the head ringmaster of his make-believe circus.

I blew him a kiss through the open window as the cab driver pulled away from the club. As Danny's expression faded into the darkness, I settled back in my seat but kept the window down. The salty night air flooded the backseat, and I took in a deep breath.

There was something so relaxing about the night sky full of stars. They glittered against the backdrop, and for a moment, I found myself wanting to make a wish. I wanted to believe that all I had to do was close my eyes and my life could be something different than it was.

I snorted as I opened my eyes and shook my head. Who was I kidding? There was nothing more to me than my desire to hold the mayoral position. That was who I was born to be. From the moment I left my mother's womb, Dad had the scepter looming in front of me as he waited to fully pass it over.

If I walked up to him and told him that I wanted to be someone else, he would laugh and then schedule an appointment for me to see a shrink.

No. My future—my destiny—was to be the mayor of Magnolia. Nothing else.

The iron gate that led to our driveway creaked as it opened. At the sound, my entire body stiffened as it sensed what was coming next. Mom and Dad, with their disappointed looks and sighs, waited for me on the other side of the solid oak front door.

The driver stopped in the middle of the wraparound driveway and glanced over his shoulder. "This the place?" he asked.

I nodded as I grabbed out a few twenties and handed them over. I contemplated asking him to drive me around a little longer, but when I saw the drapes in the front room shift, I knew Mom had seen me. If I left, our conversation was going to linger when I finally did come back.

Where were you? Don't you know that you have to be up early tomorrow? Your father set up an appointment for you, and you not being home at a decent hour is disrespectful.

I sighed as I shook Mom's voice from my mind. If I wanted to survive the ten-step walk from the front door to the stairs, it was best that I get out now.

"Thanks," I said as I pulled on the door release and slipped out of the cab. The driver seemed in a hurry to get out of here as he pulled out from behind me, and I didn't blame him.

I stood in the driveway, staring up at the massive two-story house in front of me. Even from the outside, it felt cold and manipulating. The stone exterior was harsh and uninviting. Not unlike my life.

I was ridiculous.

Taking in a deep breath, I made my way up the walkway and to the front door. Before I could even grab the handle, the door swung open and Mom was standing there. Her eyebrows were raised, and her lips parted in the question I could repeat with impeccable precision.

"Where were you?"

I sighed as I stepped into the foyer. Mom didn't move to let me in, so my arm brushed hers. A cold shiver rushed across my skin as I walked over to the center table and dropped off my purse.

Why had they come home? If I had my way, they would forever be banished to Italy. Having them here was more stressful than taking care of this ten-room house by myself.

"I was out for book club," I said as I slipped off my stilettos. My feet ached as they stretched out against the marble floor. The coolness of the stone permeated my muscles, and I felt my body relax—well, as much as I could with Mom shooting daggers in my direction.

"Do they serve alcohol at your book club?" Mom asked as she made a point of pinching her nose.

I sighed—loudly and pointedly. "What do you think? There are literally movies about how a book club *really* works." I reached up and pulled out my hairclip, causing my red, curly hair to cascade down around my shoulders.

"You shouldn't be drinking. Dad set up a breakfast with the Kerstons, and we can't have you hung over. He has the potential to be a big donor for your campaign."

I turned away from Mom and closed my eyes. I gathered my strength to bolster my patience, which was beginning to wane. "I'll be fine," I said through gritted teeth.

"But—"

"I'm headed to bed." I made my way across the foyer and to the stairs. I took them two at a time, despite Mom's loud protest. Once I was on the second level, I padded over to my room and shut my door.

When I was safely inside, I leaned against the wall and drew in a deep breath.

In and out. In and out, I chanted to myself as I forced my breath to match my mantra. It was a technique Sawyer taught me to do when I was overwhelmed. And lately, I was becoming more and more overwhelmed.

It took a few deep breaths, but my anxiety finally lessened. With the world around me settling, I pushed off the wall and made my way into my bathroom. I was going to take a hot bath complete with a bath bomb. Then I was going to curl up under my comforter with a book and read until I passed out.

Tomorrow, I'd face the life my parents had picked out for me. Tomorrow, I'd be responsible Victoria.

But tonight, I was going to be me.

Tonight, I wasn't going to worry about the polls or my constituents.

Tonight, I was going to be free.

3

SHARI

The club was not my normal scene, but I was intent on trying to redefine what my normal was. I wasn't married Shari anymore, but I also wasn't young Shari. However, I was determined that lonely, stuck with cats, knitting Shari wasn't an option, so I decided that I was going to climb out of the shell I'd lived in since marrying my high school boyfriend and find who Shari was.

And even though I was pretty certain that I wasn't going to see any of these club goers in the future, there was no time like the present. If I couldn't at least have a conversation with a stranger here, I was stopping by the craft store on the way home and leaning into crazy cat lady.

"See anyone who peeks your interest?" Clementine asked as she sidled up next to me.

I was leaning against the back wall, watching everyone around me. Men moved by me too quickly, and it was getting harder and harder to tell any of them apart. I shrugged and glanced over at Clementine, whose cheeks were pink from exertion. She was having fun dancing with the girls and handing her business card out at the same time.

She looked happy. Happier than I'd seen her in a long time. And she had that kind of happiness that made me jealous. Painfully jealous.

"Eh," I said as I sighed and folded my arms. Was I crazy? Dating, really? I was pretty sure no man here wanted to see my stretch marks from two children or my suddenly sagging boobs. I wasn't young and perky like some of these girls. And yet, I was the idiot who'd thought that coming here might actually make me feel better.

"I kind of want to go home," I said as I tucked my hair behind my ear in an attempt to keep my emotions in check. I wanted to break down, but I doubted sniffling and crying would help my saggy middle-aged mom appearance. If I wanted to save face, I needed to leave with as much dignity as I had left.

"No," Clementine said a little too quickly. She grabbed my hand, and her cheeks flushed a deeper red. "You can't go until you at least talk to a guy." She scanned the room and then stopped. She raised her hand and pointed in the direction of a group of guys. They were laughing and drinking beers.

I sighed, not wanting to tell Clementine that I was pretty sure I wasn't their type. I'd seen them earlier, and they had a string of blonde, skinny, and, most importantly, *young* girls coming in and out of their circle. The last thing they wanted was a middle-aged vice principal coming in and breaking up their party.

"What?" Clementine asked as she turned to face me. "You're hot and sexy." Then she grabbed my shoulders and leaned in like we were doing a two-person huddle. "You need this, Shari. You need to get the confidence that you lost when *the loser who shall not be named* cheated."

I stared into her dark eyes, listening to her words. I knew she meant well, but she didn't know. She didn't understand the situation I was in. Not only was my body an insecurity, but I also wasn't flying solo. I came with two little side dishes—one of which was determined to spoil the meal.

The guys she was pointing at looked young and free. The only thing I had to offer was to clip their wings as they became a father to two little kids.

"It's not a marriage, it's a conversation," Clementine said as if she could read my mind.

I glanced over at her to see her offer me an encouraging smile. Dread and fear filled my stomach. Was I really going to do this? Was I going to put myself out there?

A few of the guys from the group peeled off, leaving a dark-haired guy who was laughing with his bleach-blond, tanned friend. Dark-haired guy was drinking a beer, and the surfer man was throwing darts into the dartboard behind them.

I could do this. I wrangled hordes of children all the time. How was this any different? They were two men. If I couldn't handle this, I might as well quit now.

Fear clung to me like the cloud over Eeyore, and I was beginning to doubt the sun even shone above it. "But—"

"No buts. Go or I'm never babysitting again." Clementine narrowed her eyes as if she wanted to show me that she meant business.

I glared at her. "Hitting me where it hurts. No fair."

Clementine shrugged. "You need some motivation, and I'm nothing if not happy to oblige. I'm just helping you out here, sister."

I chuckled at her choice of words. With the way my brother, Jake, looked at her, I was pretty sure *sister* wasn't too far off. They were going to get married. It was only a matter of time. Before I could wonder if she knew Jake's intention, she turned me and shoved me in the direction of dark-haired guy and surfer man.

Surfer man was laughing at something dark-haired guy said. I sucked in my breath and headed in their direction. I could do this. I could. I was confident—er, resilient. When they rejected me, which I was sure they would, I was going to bounce back. After all, I had some experience in rejection. What was one more?

At least then Clementine would be appeased.

Just as I approached the two men, surfer guy said something to brown-hair guy and, a second later, passed by me, leaving brown-haired guy alone. I paused as brown-haired guy pulled out his phone and started swiping at the screen.

Panic rose up inside of me as I stood there, in the middle of traffic, trying to figure out if I would keep going and interrupt him or if I would turn and run like the devil out of this place.

I should have never come. This was a giant mistake.

"Excuse me," someone said at the same time they shoved into my shoulder. My stilettos were no match for the force the person exerted on me, and suddenly, I went flying forward...right into brown-haired guy.

I tried to keep myself from toppling onto him. I did, but I failed. I yelped as my body flung itself onto his. He let out a *humph*, and the sound of his phone clattering on the ground caused me to close my eyes.

Maybe if I pretended that his incredibly strong arms weren't around me right now, literally holding me up, or that my hands weren't currently pressed against his pecs, or that he smelled like the ocean and spice, then I just might be able to survive this ordeal.

"You okay?" His deep voice filled the air between us. It was soft and smooth and inches from my ear, which only reminded me further of how close we were together.

"Yep, mmhmm," I mumbled as I moved to push off him and stand. But I hadn't expected how tangled my legs and shoes were, and just as I pulled back, I lost my balance and toppled into him once more.

He seemed much more ready to catch me this time as his hands wrapped around my arms and kept me upright. "I'm not so sure," he said with a slight chuckle to his voice.

As if he feared what I might do if I tried to walk again, he half guided, half lifted me up and onto a barstool next to him. With my fight with gravity solved, I took a moment to take a few deep breaths and gain my composure before I was going to look back up at him.

My cheeks were on fire, and my entire body was shaking from embarrassment. This was not how I saw my return into the dating world going, nor did I have the confidence that I could finish up this interaction on a good note.

"Everything okay?" I heard Brett ask from behind me.

"Maybe a water?" Brown-haired guy asked.

"I'm okay," I said, quickly raising my face, and in doing so, I discovered just how close brown-haired guy was to me. He was inches away as he leaned across the counter toward Brett.

My entire stomach flip-flopped as I swallowed against the lump in my throat. Brown-haired guy turned to look at me. His dark eyes were caramel colored with flecks of gold in them. His wavy hair had shifted and fell across his forehead, and his lips were tipped up into a half smile that got my heart racing.

Then I realized that I was staring at his lips, and embarrassment helped me crash down into reality. Not

wanting him to notice my stare or, if he had, hopefully
distract him from what that meant, I dropped my gaze to
my hands and stared at them as if they had the answer to
my predicament.

"Danny."

His deep voice drew my gaze up to find him leaning
closer to me with his hand extended. He'd rested his other
hand behind me and was using it to hold himself up. I was
caged between the counter behind me and his very broad
and, from what I could tell from his t-shirt, very muscular
chest.

"Danny?" I asked, not sure what he meant by that.

"My name, it's Danny." He wiggled his fingers in
front of me as if he were waiting for me to take his
hand.

I cleared my throat and nodded. "Oh." Then I shook
his hand for a second before dropping my hand back into
my lap and clasping it.

He smiled, exposing his white, perfect teeth. Geez,
everything about this guy was pure perfection. It made me
feel small and even more incompetent that I'd thought I
could somehow measure up to him. Coming over here
had been a mistake. A huge, colossal mistake.

Then he slowly leaned into me until we were almost
cheek to cheek. I could feel the warmth emanating from
his chest, and his cologne was intoxicating as I breathed it
in. It felt as if the entire world was slowing and all that
existed was he and I.

"This is when you tell me your name," he said slowly.

His voice sounded as smooth as chocolate, and I found myself leaning into him with a desire to consume more.

It had been a long time since a man had stood this close to me. Since a man was this gentle. He talked to me in a way that sent shivers up my spine and exploding through my body.

"I do?" I asked before I could police my own words. My voice was breathy, and my skin flushed with embarrassment.

This guy was good. *Danny* was good. He knew just the right things to reel a woman in. And I was caught. Hook, line, and sinker.

He pulled back and nodded. His perfectly formed lips were closed, and he was staring at me. He didn't drop my gaze. And try as I might, I didn't see any sign of disgust in the look he was giving me. He looked genuine. Like, somehow this man wanted to know who I was.

Me.

And then I paused. I wanted to tell him my name, I did. But then fear grew inside of me, and suddenly, the last thing I wanted was to be sitting here, next to him. I needed to get out of here. Now.

"I'm going," I murmured as I pushed off the counter and hurried over to Clementine and Maggie. They were leaning against the table, looking delightfully buzzed. Thankfully, just as I approached the table, Fiona joined us, and I quickly gathered them around me and ushered them toward the door.

For a moment, before I was out of sight, I paused and

turned to take one last look at Danny. He was leaning effortlessly against the counter, propped up by his elbow. His jaw was moving up and down, and even in the dim light of the club, I could see his muscles working. He tossed a few more peanuts into his mouth, and he looked so at ease.

Not the jumbled mess of emotions that was my current state. I studied him, reveling in the satisfaction that I'd actually talked to a man who was not my husband. I could check that off my bucket list. Now I could put this whole dating idea behind me and move forward with the knowledge that I wasn't meant to be with anyone.

My future held Bella and Tag in it, and that was it.

"Why are we leaving?" Maggie asked as she leaned against my shoulder. She was tipsy, and I had to use my arm and side to help hold her up.

Just as I turned to focus on her, Danny brought his gaze up to meet mine. For some reason, as soon as he caught me, I couldn't look away. Instead, I stood there like an idiot, staring at him.

His sexy half smile returned, and he tipped his head forward, using two fingers to salute me. My entire body responded in a way that I'd thought had died years ago. Back when Craig acted as if the sheer sight of my body repulsed him.

The fact that a man—and an attractive man at that— was taking the time to acknowledge me had me aching for touch. The ache to be pulled into someone's warm arms and held like I was all that mattered in the world returned to me full force.

Maggie hiccuped, and I pulled my attention away from Danny and back over to her. I shook my head a few times, hoping that would dislodge those thoughts and desires.

I was a mom with two children and a household to run. I was a vice principal. I was an adult who had to pay her mortgage and health insurance. I was pretty sure I was not what this man wanted. He seemed carefree and single. The last thing he wanted was for a woman like me to come into his life and drag him down.

I was a fool to think that I could offer him anything. I was a fool to allow the desire for him—or any man—to fester inside of me.

I hurried Maggie, Clementine, and Fiona out of the club and into the night air. I was going to forget this night and how Danny made me feel. I was going to forget the thought that I just might want something more for myself. That I had this deep desire inside of me that ached to be someone more than Shari, vice principal and mom of two. That there was this woman inside of me who was begging to be released. And I couldn't help but wonder if Danny could be the one to help release her.

And then I felt like an idiot. Danny wasn't the gate-keeper to my happiness. I was just a woman who embarrassingly fell all over him in her effort to flirt. He'd been nice to me because he was a gentleman, not because he was attracted to me.

I wasn't going to be anyone more than who I already

was. It was foolish to think otherwise, and right now, the last thing I could afford to be was a fool. Too many people depended on me, and I was determined to not let them down.

Ever.

4

VICTORIA

Morning came too soon.

Mom was in a panic and not quiet about her worries. She woke me by coming into my room and banging all of my dresser drawers shut after she opened them. She was searching for something, but I had no idea what.

I cursed in my mind as I sat up and rubbed my eyes. The sun was barely peeking through the blinds, and it was way too early to be awake on a Saturday.

"Ma," I said, wincing at the bite in my tone that I hadn't been able to keep at bay.

Mom turned to stare at me. She looked shocked at the tone I used, but she had to be joking. She was in my room at six in the morning.

"I need my curling iron, and I know you like to take it," she said as she moved past my bed and into my bathroom.

I sighed as I pulled my covers off my legs and stood.

There was no way I was going back to bed now. Mom was stressed, and if I pulled the blankets over my head and attempted to shut her out, I would pay for it with her passive aggressive sighs the rest of her stay here.

If I wanted to survive their return, I needed to be the doting daughter that I'd always been. This was not the time to attempt to reinvent myself. Right now, everything needed to stay the same. For my sanity, and for Mom's.

"Did you check your closet?" I asked as I folded my arms across my chest and leaned against the doorjamb of the bathroom. I watched as she pulled open all of my vanity's drawers, shuffled a few things around, and then slammed them in pursuit of the next drawer.

When she turned up empty-handed, she straightened and stared me down. "What did you do with it?"

I sighed and motioned to my naturally curly hair. "I don't use curling irons. I didn't take it."

Mom's eyebrows shot up as her lips pursed. A signature look she'd perfected since I was a kid.

I hated that, even though I was in my thirties, my mom still saw me as a child. I hated that I was under the thumb of parents who still thought that they controlled me.

I needed my own place.

"Did you bring one back with you?" I asked with the calmest voice I could muster.

Mom scowled at me. "The European plug won't work on our sockets, and I left my other one in the D.C. house." She blew out her breath as she rested her hands on her hips. "I guess I'll have Caroline go out and buy one before she gets here."

I tried not to roll my eyes at my mom's blatant disrespect for our housekeeper. "Caroline is here to clean, not run your errands," I said.

Mom stared me down. "What does that mean?"

There was no way my mom didn't see how rude she was being. I parted my lips to explain myself but then paused. I may have been known as Magnolia's fiercest competitor since I was in high school, but any brawl with my mother would be ugly. If I wanted her to keep to her space and allow me to stay in mine, I needed to pick my words carefully.

"How about I get dressed and run over to Clementine's. Her store isn't open yet, but I'm sure she'll let me in."

I could watch in real time as Mom's cheeks went from red to pink and then to their natural color. She took in a deep breath and sighed. "I think I can handle that."

I nodded as I started pushing her toward my bedroom door. "Well, then, you need to leave so I can get dressed."

Thankfully, Mom didn't fight me as I ushered her toward the hallway. Just as I began to shut the door, she called out my name.

"Tori," she said softly.

I winced at the nickname only my family was allowed to call me. But instead of asking her for the millionth time not to call me that, I forced a smile. "Yes?"

She motioned toward my face and hair. "Make sure to fix yourself before you head out."

Insert internal groan.

"I mean, you are the mayor. You have a standard to uphold." She gave me a curt nod and then turned and disappeared down the stairs.

Now alone, I decided to do something completely juvenile and stuck my tongue out in her direction. Call it immaturity. Call it channeling my inner teenager. Whatever it was, I needed to decompress, and that was the first thing that came to mind.

Feeling somewhat satisfied with myself, I hurried back into my room and shut the door. After a hot shower, I stood in front of the steam-filled mirror and sighed. Regret for what I'd said this morning hung around me like the humidity in the room.

To say that Mom and I had a challenging relationship was an understatement. I knew she struggled and had her own personal ghosts in her closet. I hated to say that broken people had a tendency to break people—because what did that say about me?—but when it came to Pamela Holt, that was the truth. She had been hurt, so it was inevitable that she would hurt me.

I sighed as I yanked my wide-tooth comb through my damp hair. After running some curl-calming cream across the strands, I moved to my makeup. Just as I finished applying the last swipe of mascara, my phone chimed.

I stuck the wand back into the container, tossed it in my Caboodle that I'd had since the mid-nineties, and hurried out of the bathroom, shutting the light off as I went.

Once I located my phone, I swiped it on and read the text from Sawyer.

Sawyer: You up? Your dad wants to have breakfast with Kerston Pharmacy this morning. They're a big donor —in case you forgot.

I sighed as I nodded along with my fingers as I typed out my response.

Me: I haven't forgotten. I know they are big. I'm up and getting dressed.

Sawyer sent me back a thumbs-up and then the address of the country club across the bridge. I sent him back a GIF of a saluting man and then tossed my phone onto the bed.

After dressing in a white button-down top tucked into a pair of teal dress pants, I slipped into my heels, grabbed my purse, and headed out of my room.

The house was quiet as I descended the stairs and headed into the kitchen. Even though our meeting would most likely involve food, I needed coffee if I was going to survive the next few hours.

While the coffee pot was humming, I slipped out my phone and located my brother's number. I was excited that he was back in town—but I was more excited by the fact that he would take the heat off me. If I wasn't the only Holt in a thirty-mile radius, Mom would be able to nitpick someone else.

And with my lackluster poll numbers, I needed her to

distract me as little as possible.

Me: When are you coming home? I need some help here.

I waited a few seconds for him to respond and then felt like a dork. Knowing his record, he'd stayed out until the sun came out. He was most likely passed out on someone's couch with his phone buried under him or under his latest fling's clothing.

His lack of response left my mind as the coffee machine chimed. Needing to get moving with my day, I slipped my phone into my purse and busied myself with filling my traveler's mug with coffee and screwing on the top.

I didn't bother saying goodbye to Mom. I doubted she was up anymore. Knowing her, she was back in bed with the covers pulled around her neck, her desperate need for a curling iron completely forgotten.

After climbing into my car, I headed down the streets of Magnolia on my way to Clem's place. The sun was peeking out over the horizon, and the sky was covered with shades of orange and purple. All of those colors were a striking contrast against the deep blue of the ocean water.

If I wasn't so stressed about my life and this election, I might have taken a minute to enjoy the view. But slowing down only meant falling behind, and there was no way I was going to lose this election.

I *had* to win.

I parked behind the hardware store and headed to the back door. After a few jiggles, I was able to angle the door just right to slip the door open—a skill I'd learned from the few times I'd hung out with Clementine while growing up and her father had forgetfully locked the door.

I held my purse to my side as I climbed the stairs. After three solid knocks on her apartment door, I waited for her to answer. When she didn't respond right away, I knocked again.

"You better be the police." Her groggy voice spoke from the other side as I heard the deadbolt unlock and the door cracked open.

I mustered my best political smile as she stared at me with her brows furrowed. It took a few good blinks for her to register who I was.

"Victoria?" she asked as she allowed the door to fall open.

I nodded. "Yes. It's me."

She stared at me. "How…why…?"

Realizing that this was going to take longer than I had time for, I decided that taking charge was the best option. "I need to grab a curling iron."

"A curling iron"—she glanced behind her—"at six thirty in the morning?"

"Yes." Then I sighed. Maybe if I told her why, she'd take some pity on me. "My mom needs it, and if I don't get one, she'd make our housekeeper go out for it." I clasped my hands together. Normally I was completely against begging, but desperate times called for desperate measures.

Clementine's gaze moved from my face, down to my hands, and then back up to my face. After a few seconds, she sighed, reached up to the wall next to her, and grabbed a set of keys.

"Fine," she grumbled as she padded out of her apartment and down the stairs.

She was wearing dark-blue pajama bottoms that were well worn and a white t-shirt. Her hair was pulled up into a messy bun, and a few chunks had fallen out. I thought about teasing her but decided against it. After all, she was doing me a favor, and later this week, I was going to ask her to do me a few more favors—namely put my campaign sign in her window.

I needed to be on Clem's good side if I was going to accomplish that.

She opened the shop, motioned to the back where the household appliances were, and then slipped onto the stool behind the counter. I followed her gesture until I got to the aisle where the curling irons were stocked. They weren't the highest quality, but they would tide Mom over for now.

When I got back to Clementine, she had her head buried in the crook of her arm as she rested it on the countertop. I set the box down and rapped a few times next to her. "I'm ready."

"Thank goodness," she said as she straightened. "Ten fifty."

I pulled out my wallet and threw her a ten and a five. "Keep the change."

"I would think so." She tucked the bills next to the register and stood. "Think you can see yourself out?"

I nodded.

She didn't wait for my response. Instead she stood and stumbled over to the back door and up the back stairs. I waved to her but doubted that she saw me. As I walked out into the crisp morning air, I made a mental note to bring her a doughnut from Freya's Bakery in Newport. Clem adored their cronuts.

It took me thirty minutes to get back home, drop off the curling iron, refill my coffee, and wave at Caroline as I walked back out the door. She asked me why I was leaving so soon, but I didn't wait to respond. Instead, I shut the door on her words, knowing that if I didn't leave now, I was going to be late. And Dad did not like late.

The ride across the bridge was quiet. I thought about turning on the radio but then decided against it. As soon as I got into Newport, my phone chimed.

Once I was safely stopped at a red light, I pulled my phone from my purse only to discover that Danny had texted back.

Danny: You're not making me want to come back.

He punctuated his sentence with a laughing emoji. I rolled my eyes and texted back.

Me: You're a Holt. You need to be here to take some of the heat.

The light turned green, and I waited until I was

stopped at another red light before I picked up my phone to read his comment.

Danny: And that's why I've stayed away from Magnolia. Being a Holt sucks when you live there.

I shook my head as I pressed on the gas and flipped on my blinker. I paused as I took a left and drove until I hit the country club. I was now five minutes late. After I parked, I grabbed my purse, shoved open the door, and hurried across the parking lot. The hostess was waiting for me as she held open the large glass door.

I gave her a quick smile, and she motioned toward the left. "Conference room B," she called after me as I half ran, half walked down the hall.

Once I got to the door, I paused and took a deep breath. I forced a smile a few times until my cheeks felt warmed up enough to perform that task effortlessly on their own. I patted down my windblown hair and straightened my shirt.

Just as I reached out to grab the door handle, my phone chimed again. I reached into my purse and glanced down at the text Danny had just sent me.

A real Victoria Holt smile spread across my lips as I read what he wrote.

Danny: Fine. See you this evening

5

SHARI

I was too old to stay out like I had the night before. When the sun crept into my room, every portion of my body ached. My joints, my feet, my head. I groaned as I flipped to my back and covered my face with my arm.

I was never allowing Fiona to suggest what we should do ever again. She was young and spry. I was a divorcée with two children. To think that I was just going to blend into the club crowd and not feel the effects the next morning was a joke.

I belonged at home in my pajamas with a bottle of wine and the newest cheesy Hallmark movie. If I was going to be single, I might as well lean into that lifestyle.

Besides, if I had been home instead of at the club, I wouldn't have made a total fool of myself in front of Danny. I wouldn't have to pretend to be someone I wasn't. I didn't hit on guys. I didn't flirt. Apparently, when I tried, my fate was

for my efforts to end up exactly like they had last night...
with me falling on my face and making a fool of myself.

A gigantic, horrible fool of myself.

I was an idiot.

"Mommy!" Bella screamed as my door swung open
and slammed against the wall. Bella didn't seem to notice
as she sprinted across the room and dive-bombed my bed.

I was attempting to slip my arm under me so I could
sit up, but I was too slow. With Bella on my bed, she was
pinning my arm between the comforter and mattress.

Not having the energy to wiggle her to the side so I
could free my arm, I collapsed back onto the bed and
closed my eyes. Being a mom took too much effort
sometimes.

"Good morning." She giggled. I could tell from the
closeness of her voice and the smell of Fruity Pebbles that
she was inches from my face.

I cracked open an eye and couldn't help but grin at my
precocious daughter who stared back at me. Not wanting
to spend any more time wallowing in my self-pity, I
opened both eyes and grinned back at her.

"Good morning." I wiggled my free arm out from
under the covers and used it to pin her to the bed. Then I
moved far enough away to free my other arm, and a tick-
ling party ensued.

Bella screamed and giggled as she tried to wiggle away
from me. When she was belly laughing and wheezing that
she was going to pee, I finally let up. I relaxed against my

headboard as she scurried into my bathroom and shut the door.

After Bella returned, she turned on my TV and settled in with a cartoon while I grabbed my phone from my nightstand and lost myself for a few minutes on social media. Once I was pretty sure I was turning into a slug, I peeled myself off the bed and padded into the bathroom to take a long and hot shower.

I felt refreshed and ready to forget the night before and all the embarrassment that had come with it. I pulled my wet hair up into a bun at the top of my head, dressed in an oversized t-shirt and skinny jeans, and then clicked off the TV, much to Bella's chagrin.

I ate breakfast as Bella sat at the counter, chatting my ear off. Just as I set my dishes in the sink, Tag pulled open his door and stumbled into the kitchen. His hair was disheveled, and he was still wearing his clothes from the day before. Jake had told me that he'd asked Tag to change, but that child didn't seem willing to, so Jake didn't push it.

I didn't blame him. I would have let it slide as well.

I gave Tag a wide smile, but he didn't respond. Instead he walked straight to the kitchen cupboard and pulled out a Pop-Tart. He looked like he was going to sprint back into his room, so I moved to stand in front of him and get his attention.

"Hey," I said.

Tag kept his gaze on the silver-colored packaging.

"I'm thinking we can go out and do some school shopping," I said as I dipped down to meet his gaze.

Tag shrugged, probably realizing that if he didn't speak to me, I wasn't going to let up. "Fine. Whatever," he said as he sidestepped me and hurried into his room.

Satisfied with his answer, I clapped my hands and then waved toward Bella. "Go. Get dressed. We're heading out."

———

An hour into our shopping excursion at the mall, I realized that it was a huge mistake. Instead of this being a fun family outing, it had turned sour, fast. Tag was annoyed with Bella because she wanted to try on every piece of clothing before she decided on her new school wardrobe. And on the flip side, Bella was annoyed with Tag because all he wanted to do was stare at the video games in the gaming store.

Having two different gendered children who were both stubborn and bullheaded was hard. I attempted to cool them down through compromise, but nothing worked. They were both determined to hate the other until the end of time.

I sighed as I glanced out the store window to where Tag was fuming as he sat on a nearby bench. Bella was busy singing to herself in the dressing room as she tried on the stack of dresses she'd picked out. I was really trying to let each child have their freedom. After my separation with Craig, I hated how I had to be the bad and good guy.

And if I were honest with myself, I was mostly the bad guy. Or that's how it felt.

I pushed my hands through my hair and tipped my face upwards, allowing my eyes to close. The fluorescent lights shone through my lids, but there was something calming about the glowing pink that I saw. Here, I could block out the world. Here, I wasn't Mom.

Thoughts of Danny floated back into my mind, and despite the fact that I knew I should push out his brown floppy hair and sexy grin, I couldn't. He was intriguing and, for a moment, made me feel like Shari, the woman. It had been a long time since I'd felt like Shari, the woman.

"I'm done, Mommy," Bella sang.

I righted my head just in time to catch all of the dresses that she'd chucked in my direction. I gave her an exasperated look, but she didn't seem to acknowledge me. She danced around as I dumped her clothes into the cart and hurried to the cash register.

"Where's Tag?" Bella asked as the teenager behind the counter started scanning the tags.

I glanced behind me in the direction I'd seen Tag last… only to see that he was gone. I cursed under my breath.

"You shouldn't say naughty words," Bella scolded as she reached up and waggled a finger at me.

I shot her an *I'm sorry* smile and then turned back to the cashier with the hopes that she would get moving faster. "If we could speed this up…"

The cashier gave me an annoyed look as she held the tag up and then slowly put the scanner to the barcode.

"Okay," I said, weighing the desire to ask for the manager against the desire to catch up with my son.

After what felt like a million years, the cashier handed me my receipt, which I snatched from her hand as I grabbed the handles of the plastic bag and pulled it from the counter. Then I held onto Bella's hand as I hurried from the store and out into the walkway.

Newport Mall was busy for a Saturday. Families were weaving in and out of the stores. Walking groups were chatting and glaring at the clumps of teenagers that took up large amounts of floor space. I rose up on my toes as I attempted to scan everyone's face.

Tag had to be here somewhere.

With the bag of clothes in one hand and Bella's hand firmly grasped in my other, I pushed through the crowds in search of my child.

We stopped at the arcade first. When he wasn't there, I pulled Bella from the racing game—much to her chagrin —and headed back out to the walkway. Thankfully, it was nearing lunchtime, so most people had headed to the food court, which lessened the crowds I had to look through.

By the time we got to the gaming store, I was sweaty and puffing. I slipped my hand from Bella's and told her to search the left side of the store while I searched the right. Bella nodded, and soon, I was peeking down each aisle in search of my son.

It didn't take long for me to find him. I let out a sigh of relief as anger flooded my veins. Tag was talking to an older guy—most likely an employee—while holding the plastic case of a game up in the air. Despite seeing red, all I could focus on was getting my son and getting him home. Then, I would decide on a punishment for him.

With the way I was feeling, removal of his gaming system from his room seemed like the right kind of recompense for this crime.

"Tag, why on earth did you leave?" I asked as I approached him. I wanted to fight the anger in my voice, I did, but my emotions felt as if they were bubbling over. When I got to him, I reached out and wrapped my hand around his arm. I feared that if I didn't hold onto him, he was going to sprint away, again.

"Mom," Tag said is his perfectly rehearsed teenager whine. He lifted his arm as if that was all it would take to break my hold on him. "I'm fine," he hissed as he turned to glare back at me.

"We've been searching the entire mall for you. All you had to do was wait a few more minutes and then we could have come here together."

Tag groaned and twisted, but I wasn't going to let go. Not with this attitude.

"I'm sorry. I think I may have distracted him with questions." The deep and slightly familiar voice of the man Tag had been talking to startled me.

Fearing that I might actually know the owner of that voice—and fearing that he knew and remembered me—my entire face heated when I was met with the soft, gold-flecked eyes of Danny.

Danny.

Oh crap, it was Danny.

"Wha...I mean...why...?" Great. My brain was short circuiting. A master's degree and years as a teacher hadn't prepared me to run into the man I'd literally fallen into last night.

Could my life get any worse?

"Hey." The way he said that simple word made me blush. Suddenly, I was the geeky teenager losing her mind because the quarterback on the football team was paying attention to *me*.

Ugh. I needed to crawl into a hole and die.

"We should get going," I said as I held onto Tag and started pulling him toward the door. Tag felt like a dead-weight as he dug his heels in. He shoved the game he'd been holding into my face, and I knew what he wanted.

There was no way I could purchase this game for my child who had just run off. But I also didn't want Danny to be privy to the tantrum that would ensue if I told Tag no.

After a split second of waffling, I finally decided that being a good mother was better than looking good, and I took the game from Tag. "We'll discuss this when we get home. But right now, with your current behavior, a new game is out of the question."

I didn't wait to see what Tag was going to do. Instead, I tightened my grip and half walked, half dragged Tag to the front of the store. The world around me seemed foggy as embarrassment coursed through my veins.

I was pretty sure that Danny was staring at me. I was pretty sure the entire store was staring at my preteen as he screamed at me. The words he was using made my face flush, and all I wanted was for a hole to open up and swallow me whole.

This was not where I wanted to be. This was not the life I would choose for myself. For a moment, as I stood there with my hand around my bratty child, waiting for Bella to join us, I wanted to return to the other night. When all I was worried about was acting like a fool in front of Danny.

Back when I wasn't worried about a mortgage, my two little humans, or my crumbling reputation.

Instead, I was here at the mall, where my child was making a fool of me in front of the first guy who had caused my heart to race in years. The first guy whom I wanted to know more about.

Why did fate hate me like she did?

The moment I saw Bella, I waved to her and headed out to the walkway. Once she caught up with me, I didn't stop until I was in the parking lot and in search of my car. Of course, I hadn't paid attention to where we parked, and all the cars had changed since we got here.

It was like trying to find a needle in a haystack. I raised my key fob and clicked it a few times.

Nothing.

We moved to the next row of cars.

Click. Nothing.

Crap.

Thankfully, Tag had quieted to a moody mumble. Bella was singing softly to herself. And I was sweating. My entire body felt sticky despite the cooling temperature. I'm sure I looked like a half-crazed woman as we wandered the parking lot in search of my car.

"Can I help?"

I yelped and turned, only to find Danny standing behind me with a ridiculous grin across his lips. He was holding a paper bag and looking chipper. I wanted to run and hide behind the blue minivan next to me, but I also didn't want to look like a fool—which I was pretty sure he thought I was anyway.

"I'm good," I whispered and moved to get away from him.

"Are you sure?" he asked as he fell in step with me. "I'm great at finding lost cars."

I glanced at him, sweeping my gaze over his long legs and ridiculously toned torso. T-shirt makers really knew how to fashion their material so it covered yet hinted to the muscles underneath.

My temperature spiked at the thought of Danny's muscles.

Yes, Danny was fit. He was young and, from the looks of it, had no worries. I, on the other hand, was covered in stretch marks and enjoyed weekends filled with chocolate and wine. We were on different planets. He was on the hot, young, and fit planet, where I was on the single-mom planet.

Never shall the two meet.

"I bet you are," I said as I hiked my purse strap higher up onto my shoulder. "But I'm almost there." To my satisfaction, when I raised my arm one more time and clicked the fob, my car beeped and the rear lights flashed.

All I needed to do was walk down ten cars, and I would be safe from this man.

"See," I said triumphantly as I motioned toward my car. "All good."

Danny gave me a look that said he didn't believe me, but he didn't fight me. Instead, he followed next to me as we walked toward the car. Tag distracted him by talking about whatever game they'd been discussing in the store, so I took the time to gather my thoughts and regain my composure.

Tag's outburst plus running into Danny had definitely exhausted me. I was ready to get home, get into my pajamas, and pretend that this entire day hadn't happened.

"All right, we're here," I sang out as I turned to motion for my kids to get in. Bella twirled to her door and disappeared inside. Tag lingered as he finished up his conversation with Danny and then walked past me. The slamming of his car door made me sigh.

Not wanting Danny to ask me what was wrong, I turned to smile at him. But as my gaze met his, my breath caught in my throat. He was staring down at me...smiling. Not in a creepy neighbor way or in a pity way. In a genuine way that had me wondering if he was happy to see me.

Which was weird. We weren't friends. I didn't know him, and he didn't know me. I was pretty sure as soon as I drove away from here, I was never going to see him again.

"Well, it was great running into you again," I said, and before I could stop myself, I stretched out my hand to shake his.

His gaze dipped down to my hand and then back up to meet my gaze head-on. "Really? Was it?"

What did that mean?

He must have seen my confused expression because a second later, he added, "You left in a hurry last night." He reached up to push his hand through his hair, and all I could think about was how he would look incredible in a shampoo commercial. His hair looked smooth and soft. And his muscles rippled when he moved. Craig had never had muscles like this. Like, ever.

I blinked a few times when I realized that I was full-on staring at this man. What was wrong with me? Maybe I had some strange virus that caused women to do crazy things when they were around attractive men.

I stopped my mind when it seemed to want to expound on that thought.

I did have a virus. It was called single-woman syndrome. And even though I was going through a divorce, it didn't mean that I was ignorant of the male form. Or what said male form could do to a woman.

Heat pricked at the back of my neck, and I cleared my throat in an effort to clear my head. What were we talking about?

Right. My leaving last night.

"Well, as you have now been privy to, I am a very busy person." I nodded toward my car.

Danny's gaze followed my gesture and then returned to me. "I can see that." Then he pinched his lips together as if he wanted to ask me a question but wasn't sure if he should.

I sighed and shook my head. "No. There is no Mr. in my life." Then I hurried to add. "Definitely in theirs. But their dad is no longer my husband...I'm divorced." The words left my lips in a whisper, and suddenly, my entire body went cold.

That was the first time I'd said that in front of a stranger. Everyone in Magnolia knew my relationship status, no matter if I told them or not. All the busybody women made sure to spread the news fast and far.

But here in Newport, I was a small fish in a large ocean. People didn't just know my business, and telling him tasted sour on my tongue. Those words meant failure, and I was tired of being a failure.

"I'm sorry," Danny said, snapping me from my thoughts. I turned to face him. He looked apologetic and had taken a step toward me. He reached his hand out and took my still extended hand in his.

The warmth from his skin shocked me and caused me to audibly gasp. My cheeks warmed from my response, but if Danny noticed, he didn't say anything. Instead, he leaned closer and smiled down at me.

"It's his loss..." He raised his eyebrows as if he expected me to finish his statement.

Confused about what he wanted me to do, I parted my lips, but nothing came out. How could it? With him this close to me, touching me, the only words I could form in my head were *hot man,* and I was trying will all my might to keep those thoughts inside.

"This is where you finally tell me your name."

My name. I could handle my name. After all, I'd been saying it since I could talk. One word. Nice and simple.

"Shari," I whispered.

The side of his mouth tipped up higher as he nodded. "Shari. It's nice to meet you, Shari." My name rolled off his tongue like he enjoyed the taste.

All I could do was nod, pull my hand from his, and sprint to my car. Right now, I needed out of this parking lot and out of Newport. With the way my heart was beating, my entire body yearning for touch, I was going to do something very stupid, and right now, my heart couldn't handle stupid.

Right now, I needed to keep myself safe. And that meant keeping myself away from Danny for good.

It was a pact that I needed to make with myself.

Handsome Danny was off limits.

No matter what.

VICTORIA

I never realized how exhausting golf was until I spent the entire afternoon and into the early evening playing. I tried many times to excuse myself, but Dad wasn't having it. He was determined to get the Kerstons to endorse me, even if that meant me swinging the club until my arms felt like they were going to fall off.

I was hot and sweaty when I walked into the restaurant at the country club. I pulled my gloves off and handed them, along with a twenty, to Carter, my golf caddy for the day. He took them, thanked me, and headed back outside to get started with someone else.

Dad was laughing and shaking hands with Collin Kerston. I kept to the back, making sure to smile big every time his gaze made its way over to me. If I wasn't so desperate for his endorsement, I would have allowed myself to consider him attractive. But I didn't like to mix business with pleasure.

And honestly, my life had no room for pleasure right now. Not with my election looming. I needed to focus on the task at hand, and that task was me staying the mayor. I didn't have any other options.

After Dad and Collin finished their lingering conversation, Collin stepped forward and extended his hand.

"It was good seeing you again, Mayor Holt." His perfectly formed lips tipped up into a smile as he leaned in. There was a suggestive hint to his voice that had me wondering if he meant more, but I pushed that thought from my mind.

I couldn't think like that.

"Victoria, and yes, it was good to see you too." I took his hand and shook it like my father had taught me. Not too limp but firm enough to let them know you mean business.

Collin chuckled as he nodded. "I hope to see you again soon."

He sounded like he was asking a question and making a statement at the same time. I wasn't sure what to say, so I just smiled and replied with, "Of course. Message me if you're ever in Magnolia. We can get drinks. The inn just reopened, and I've heard their new chef is to die for."

As I mentioned Brett, his face slipped into my mind. Instantly, butterflies erupted in my stomach, taking me aback. I'm sure I looked strange because when I returned my focus back to Collin, he was staring at me like he didn't know what to think.

My politician smile returned, and I gave his hand a few more shakes before I let it go.

"That sounds nice. Maybe this Friday?" he asked as he leaned in.

I furrowed my brow. "You'll be in Magnolia on Friday?"

He shrugged. "I could be persuaded to make a trip."

I studied him and then coughed. How had this happened? But, when my gaze made its way back to Dad and I saw his raised eyebrows and expectant look, I smiled and nodded. "Of course. Come on Friday and I'll show you Magnolia."

"I will," Collin said without hesitating. Then he gave me one last smile and a small wink before he turned and gave his full attention to Grayson, his assistant.

Now alone and out of the scrutiny from Collin, I let out my breath and turned to focus on Dad, who nodded toward the bar. Dad ordered a scotch, and I stuck with a Sprite. I reveled in the feeling of bubbles against my throat as I took a sip. I was exhausted, and I was ready to leave. I was ready to drop the mayoral act and let my hair down.

"That went well," Dad said as he set his scotch down on the countertop. The ice clinked as he did.

It was such a familiar sound that I was swept back to my childhood for a moment. Sitting in Dad's office as he answered phone calls and wrote press pieces. He was a workaholic, and I'd inherited that from him.

"Yes," I replied, knowing that he really wasn't having a conversation with me. He was congratulating himself. Like he always did. To my parents, their children were there for them to take credit for. It wasn't me accomplishing something. It was them.

Dad flicked his gaze over to me. "Why did you hesitate when Collin asked you to dinner?"

I winced. There was no way I wanted to talk about my political relationships with my father, much less potential actual relationships. "I'm just not sure I have the time," I said, hoping my relaxed tone would convince him.

But he didn't look swayed. "You should always have time for donors." His voice was stern, as if he were speaking to teenager Victoria, not adult Victoria. It was insulting, but what else could I do? I couldn't fight back. I just didn't have the strength.

"Yes," was all I could say. I wanted this conversation to end so that I could get out of here. I wanted to go back home, crawl into my bed, and order some lo mein. Then I would watch *Friends* until I passed out. That was my version of the perfect Saturday evening.

Not moshing at a local club.

Dad looked disinterested in talking to me more, so I gave him a quick kiss on the cheek and hurried out the door. The valet found my car in record time, and soon I was in the driver's seat, heading toward Magnolia.

The house was quiet when I got there, which I was

grateful for. That meant Mom was either out or in her room. I didn't try to search for her. If she wanted to find me, she knew where to look.

After putting in an order to Eddie Cheng's, I climbed into my oversized footie pajamas and slipped under the covers. I made sure to let Eddie know to knock loudly because the only thing that was going to get me out of bed was some chicken lo mein with pot stickers.

I turned on *Friends* and settled down on my pillows. My entire body relaxed as I pulled the covers up to my chin and let out my breath. I was so tired that every muscle ached as I released them. It was as if when I was up and walking, I held the stress of the election and the stress of my parents inside of every fiber. The only time I got some reprieve was when I forced myself to relax. That was the only time I felt like I could breathe.

That I could actually be Victoria.

Thirty minutes later, I glanced down at my phone. No Eddie yet. I clicked the screen on to see that there were no missed texts. I thought about climbing out of bed and checking to see if he'd left the food at the door… but then dismissed that thought. After all, he knew to knock loud, and it was a Saturday night. He was probably busy.

My eyes drifted closed a few times, and once I let them settle, a sound from the hallway startled me awake. I pushed myself up to sitting and peered into the darkness. Would Eddie actually enter my house if I didn't answer the door?

"Mom?" I called out, straining my ears to hear anything.

Nothing.

"Eddie?" I asked, and then felt stupid. Eddie wasn't there. I doubted breaking and entering was something a restaurant owner wanted on their record.

After a few seconds of waiting with my breath sucked in and my body on high alert, I eventually shook my head and settled back.

"Boo!"

I screamed, flailing my arms to free them from my comforter, only to find Danny's grinning face hovering in my doorway. I cursed under my breath, grabbed a pillow, and chucked it in his direction.

"Rude," he said in a mock-indignant tone. Then he held up the plastic bag full of food and wiggled his eyebrows. "I come bearing gifts."

"So you're the reason I didn't hear the knock," I said once my breath calmed and my heart stopped pounding.

Danny chuckled as he entered my room. In the other hand, he had a six-pack of beers. "Hey, I was just in the right place at the right time," he said as he tossed the beers onto the bed—right onto my legs—then he made his way to the other side of the bed and flopped down.

My whole bed shook as he took his time to get situated. While he kicked off a few extra pillows and adjusted the blankets, I opened one of the white Styrofoam containers, causing the smell of the food to waft up along with the steam.

The smell of lo mein always sent my salivary glands into overdrive. I didn't wait for him as I grabbed my chopsticks and dove in.

"Rude," Danny said again as he grabbed a pot sticker and popped it into his mouth.

I glanced over at him as I let my lo mein noodles dangle from my mouth. I shrugged and slurped them up. "I was golfing all day," I mumbled through the food.

Danny wrinkled his nose as he dug out the black plastic fork from the bag and speared a piece of chicken. "Yuck. Why would you do that?"

The *Friends* theme song sounded in the background, and I glanced over at Danny and saw him relax against the headboard. He looked so…calm. Like nothing in this world would bother him. Like he didn't have the stress of the family name on his shoulders.

For a moment, I allowed myself to wonder what that would feel like.

And then I told myself to stop wondering. That was the last thing I needed to do. My life was about being mayor. I was born to carry on the name of Holt. Having a simple, nomad life like my younger brother just wasn't in the cards for me.

I gave him a pointed look, and he nodded as he swallowed. "Mom and Dad are home." He paused and then chuckled. "And they are desirous of you to carry on the family name."

I swallowed the lo mein that I'd been chewing, wincing as it slid down my now tightening throat. It was one thing to listen to my own thoughts about my parents' expectations, it was a whole other thing to hear it come from someone else's lips. Danny had released those ideas out into the world, and there was no way I was going to be able to pull them back and stuff them into the far corners of my mind, where they could stay. Forever.

I shrugged as I shoved another forkful of food into my mouth. "It's no big deal. It's something I gotta do." I swallowed my food. "Besides, I like being mayor. Magnolia is a beautiful town."

After a few bites of my food—despite my protests—Danny settled back on the headboard and eyed me. "Really? You like it?"

I furrowed my brow and allowed my gaze to drift over to the TV, where Ross and Rachel were talking. "Yes," I said quietly.

I knew I was supposed to say triumphantly that I was born to be mayor. That this was the path I had chosen and doing anything else would make me feel unsatisfied.

And for the most part, that was true. Except when I saw Maggie in the inn or heard Clementine talk about the dance studio. They both seemed to be moving forward in their lives, doing what was truly in their heart. And I? I was stuck in this box with no way to get out.

"Uh huh," Danny said as he leaned forward and poked me in the ribs. "You can lie to Mom and Dad. You can even lie to yourself. But I know you, sis. I know you question what you want to do."

Despite my best efforts, tears clung to the edges of my

eyelids. I wanted to shoot back that I was happy and that he didn't *really* know, but I knew that would be a lie. A lie that I was pretty sure he could see through. And I didn't need him calling me out on my deception even more.

Not wanting to delve into my mind or my happiness, I decided to turn my focus back on him. I took another bite of my food and studied him. "So how long are you home for?"

Danny's smile faltered, and suddenly, the scene being played out on the TV took his attention. I swatted his arm, slightly happy that I'd made him just as uncomfortable as he'd made me.

We should probably make that the Holt family slogan: Born to Make Each Other Uncomfortable. We all seemed to be experts at it.

Danny shrugged as he shifted on the bed once more. "I dunno. I'm sure once Mom discovers that I'm back, she'll have a list for me." He flopped his bent leg onto the bed. "Like she always does."

I nodded. Truer words had never been spoken. "Yeah. Good luck with that. With my election, I get to follow Dad around, which leaves Mom…" I clicked my tongue and nodded toward him.

He glowered at me and then took a long swig of his beer. He rested his hands on his chest and closed his eyes. "I'll survive." His voice sounded just as unsure as I'd expected.

"Uh huh," I replied as I leaned back against the head-board and brought the container up to rest on my stomach while I ate. Sure, it wasn't ladylike, and I'd die if any reporter caught me like this, but there were times when I needed to just lean back and relax. And that time was now.

We fell silent as we watched *Friends*. I finished my food and set my garbage on the floor—I'd get to it tomorrow—and curled up with my pillows and soft, fuzzy blanket. Just as my body began to relax like it'd been wanting to do all night, two sets of footsteps could be heard in the hallway. Mom was complaining to Dad that he'd stayed out too late and smelled like booze.

My entire body tensed—along with Danny's—as we sat up and stared at the door. It sounded as if they were headed straight to my room, but they could also be going to their room farther down the hall.

Before either of us could jump up and run to the closet to hide, my door swung open, and Dad's pinched lips and irritated gaze swept over me. Thankfully, he only lingered on me for a moment until Mom shrieked, "Daniel!" and came barreling into my room, pushing Dad to the side.

"Hey, Mom," Danny said as he slipped off the bed and met Mom's hug with one of his own.

Dad flicked his gaze from me to Danny, and I began to realize that I might be covered with noodles and lo mein sauce. Not wanting to look the mess that I felt, I stood, brushed off my clothes, grabbed my garbage, and shoved it into the nearby plastic bag.

Thankfully, Dad didn't say anything, and a few seconds later, he focused solely on Danny. My brother had pulled back from Mom's clutches and was nodding at whatever she was saying as she blubbered on. I could only pick out bits and pieces about how she was so grateful that he was home and why did he look so skinny.

"Hey, Dad," Danny said as he extended his hand, and they shook.

"Welcome home," Dad said. His voice was deep and tense. He didn't agree with Danny's chosen lifestyle, but I knew he worried that if he was too hard on him, it would only push Danny out the door again.

Funny how things change between parents and children. Dad felt like Danny was a balloon that would slip from his clutches and float away. Whereas I was the child that he could squash into submission. Perhaps it was my fault. I'd never given him the impression that I would leave if pressured too much.

There was this undeniable desire I had to please which mixed with the undeniable desire to be successful. That meant I would stay and fight, no matter what. And Dad knew that.

"What's your plan now that you're here?" Dad asked.

"Oh hush. I just got him home. Don't be pushing him out now," Mom said as she swatted Dad's arm.

Dad didn't pay her any mind. Instead he kept his focus on Danny, who just shrugged.

"Probably find a job. I'm thinking of staying until after the election. I gotta help my big sis get her job back."

I rolled my eyes and mouthed the word *punk* in his direction.

"You know what, I heard that there's a pregnant teacher that is leaving on sabbatical soon. They're looking for someone to replace her for six weeks." Mom glanced up at Danny. "I do know someone on the school board. It'd be steady income. It would show that the Holt family is here to help the community. What do you think?"

Danny looked as if he'd swallowed a lemon, and for a moment, I doubted that he would say yes. I wanted to intervene and tell Mom that Danny just got home. He didn't need to make that choice right now. But Danny beat me to my response.

"Sure."

I blinked once. Twice. "What?" I asked. Was he serious?

"Sure," he replied, slower this time. "What else do I have going on? Plus, teaching kids will be fun." He wrapped his arm around Mom's shoulders. "You have some great ideas."

Mom giggled.

I sighed. I knew what Danny was doing and why he was the favorite. He was a smooth talker and more flexible than I could ever be. I was jealous of his ability to speak to my parents. It wasn't a quality that I held.

"I'm going to bed," I said as I flopped down and pulled the covers up over my head.

My family didn't seem to notice that I'd left the conversation. My parents focused on Danny as he led them from my room, shutting the light off and closing the door as they exited.

I knew that Danny was doing this for me. That his

willingness to go along with Mom's proposal and his dominating my parents' attention was taking the heat off of me. And I knew I should be grateful. I knew that.

But for some reason, I didn't.

I felt worse.

I felt unhappy.

And that was beginning to drain me. More than it had ever before.

SHARI

Tuesday morning, I woke excited.

It was the first day of school, and I was ready to get some normalcy back in my life. Summer break was nice. It had helped me establish myself as a single mom and divorcée, but I was ready to stop defining myself under those terms and dive headfirst into being vice principal.

Plus, Bella was jumping off the walls this morning. She rushed around in her room, trying on every dress she owned only to settle on jeans and a pink t-shirt with a tan jacket.

I smiled as I brushed her hair and fixed two pigtails. She was chatting about how Dorothy was in her class this year and how she was excited and hopeful that they would be able to sit next to each other.

I shrugged as I finished pulling her hair through her hair tie, separated the hair, and pulled it tight.

"Well, it's up to Mrs. Davis if you sit next to her or not." I patted her shoulders. "All done."

Bella was up on her feet and twirling around her room. "I know, Mommy," she said. And then she scrunched her face. "How long will she be my teacher for? She told me last week that she's having a baby." She danced over to her toy chest and pulled out one of her dolls that looked threadbare and worn.

A small twinge of sadness crept up into my chest as I watched her hug the doll to her chest and fiddle with its ratty hair. She was growing up faster than I'd like, and soon, she wasn't going to want me in her room, brushing her hair.

Soon, she was going to block me out like Tag was.

Realizing that I needed to hurry the beast along, I sighed and stood. "Mrs. Davis wanted to be with you guys the first week of school, but then it'll be a sub. She'll be back around Thanksgiving." I patted Bella's head as I walked from the room.

Talking about Mrs. Davis's impending maternity leave just caused the stress that I was already feeling to magnify. We hadn't found a long-term sub, and we were days away from needing one. Living on a small island was great for ambiance, but it was bad for trying to find a qualified substitute teacher.

Tag was out of his room and sitting at the table when I walked into the kitchen. He had his headphones on and was watching some video on his phone. I wanted to pull the headphones from his ears and demand that he turn his phone off, but I knew he would fight me.

And right now, I was fighting my own battles. I'd focus on Tag's after school started. Then, I could give him my full attention.

"Good morning," I sang out, hoping that if I made my greeting sound exciting, he would feel the same.

But that plan fell flat. He just grunted and shifted so he was no longer facing me.

I tried to remain positive as I headed to the kitchen and poured myself a cup of coffee. The hazelnut smell wafted up and tickled my nose. Once I added a splash of creamer, I leaned against the countertop and sipped on the warm liquid. It filled my mouth and warmed my body as it went down. And for a moment, I wasn't Shari, the mom. For a moment, I could let go of the stress that came from having a preteen. Right here, right now, I was me. And I was ready to be me for just a little while longer.

If only that feeling had lasted the remainder of the morning. But after getting lunches packed, rounding up my work supplies, and ushering the kids into the car, the warmth that had once filled my body had turned to ice.

The stress returned as I drove the streets of Magnolia on my way to the elementary school. So much so that I had to take in a few deep breaths to ground me.

I parked off to the side, and as soon as I pulled out the keys, Bella and Tag had their doors open and were out of the car before I could say anything. I watched as they shouldered their backpacks and sprinted up the sidewalk toward the doors. I thought about calling them back but then decided against it.

I had enough on my plate to worry about. And, inside the school, the teachers would help keep an eye on them until school started.

With my papers and briefcase in hand, I headed toward the front doors. My heels clicked on the sidewalk, and the soft fall air surrounded me and caused my hair to tickle my nose. I wiggled my nose a few times, hoping to stop the sensation, but it didn't work, so I just quickened my pace.

When I got in the office, Cassidy was there. She had the phone pinched between her cheek and shoulder. I waved at her, and she nodded in acknowledgment but then returned to her conversation. First day of school and the phones were already buzzing. I felt for Cassidy. She was our first line of defense, and I knew she took the brunt of the angry calls.

When I got into my office, I set my bag and papers down on my desk and slipped off my suit coat. I draped it on the back of my chair and took in a deep breath. Today was the start of my new life. With my job in full force and Craig officially gone, this was what the majority of my life was going to be. It felt terrifying, and yet at the same time, it felt like a giant weight had been lifted off of my shoulders.

If I could get through today, I was going to be okay.

I was sure of it.

I grabbed my mug and headed out of my office and

over to the small coffee machine that was set up in the back corner. Just as I pulled out the pot, my gaze drifted over to Kari's office. She was sitting at her desk and nodding to a man sitting with his back to me. I furrowed my brow as I straightened, still holding the pot in my hand.

Who was she meeting with?

Sure, she was my boss, but we always kept each other in the loop. The fact that she was meeting with someone and I didn't know who they were or why they were here, intrigued me.

So I finished pouring my mug of coffee, returned the pot, and then slowly walked by her window as I held my mug to my lips, enjoying the warm steam and the smell of the coffee. I tried to look nonchalant and was relieved when Kari's gaze fell on me and she lifted her hand to wave me in.

"Shari," she called, her voice muffled through the closed door.

Bingo.

I raised my hand in response and moved to push down on her handle. I stepped into the room, and the smell of familiar cologne hit me. I furrowed my brow as I racked my brain, trying to remember where I'd smelled this scent before. And then recognition dawned on me as the man in front of Kari turned, and I was faced with Danny's half smile once more.

He stared at me with his brow furrowed and then turned to look back at Kari.

"Danny?" I blurted out and then pinched my lips together when I realized that I'd spoken out loud. Now Kari was going to ask how I knew him. And I was going to have to reveal that I went to a club over the weekend. Call me crazy, but I didn't want to start having that kind of reputation around town.

I was fairly certain people had a particular impression of me already.

"Shari?" Danny asked as he stood in that sort of way that men in historical movies did. He leaned forward and extended his hand for me to shake. "I didn't know you lived in Magnolia."

"How do you two know each other?" Kari asked as she flicked her finger between the two of us.

"We don't," I said at the same time Danny said, "A club."

Heat permeated my cheeks as I peeked over at Kari and saw that she was stifling a smile. "A club?" she asked as she raised her eyebrows and met my gaze.

"It was for the book club," I murmured.

"You're part of a book club?" Danny asked.

Realizing that I was having half a conversation with two different people, I gripped my coffee mug like it was a lifeline and took two backward steps toward the door. "I'm so sorry. I interrupted what was going on here. I'll excuse myself." But before I could sprint from Kari's office, she raised her hand to stop me.

"Actually, I asked you to come in for a reason. Daniel is interviewing to be the long-term sub for Mrs. Davis."

"What?" I squeaked out. Danny was here for a job?

Why? "I thought you lived in Newport. Why are you here?"

"He's—"

"I just heard that there was an opening and applied. I don't like to think of myself as beholden to any town," he said, cutting Kari off from what she was going to say.

When I glanced back over at Kari, she just nodded and then offered me a smile.

"It's wonderful. We've been waiting for a qualified sub, and Daniel is more than qualified." She reached over her desk and offered him her hand. "Shari can show you to Mrs. Davis' room. You can shadow her for the week to figure out her schedule and what she has planned. Your official start date is next Monday."

Danny shook her hand and nodded. "Perfect." Then he turned and offered me his knee-buckling smile.

Grr. I needed to get a grip on these ridiculous reactions that kept happening when I was around him. He was going to be a teacher at my school. Even if I wanted anything to happen between us, having him employed here effectively cut off all of those thoughts. I wasn't the kind of person who dated the people I worked with.

Geez. Dated. Why the heck was I using that word? I wasn't dating Danny. Having two conversations did not equal a relationship. I needed to get my head on straight and focus.

Focus on the fact that he was here to take the long-term sub job and not the fact that his wavy hair had fallen across his forehead and my fingers ached to brush it away.

"Are you ready?" he asked, leaning forward and clasping his hands.

I nodded and turned before my traitorous cheeks heated any more. By this point, I was sure someone was going to ask me if I was feeling well. And what was I going to tell them? That I had a fever? Or that this man who I'd allowed myself to think about more than a few times had suddenly showed up at my work.

I was a fool. A giant, colossal fool. And I had no one else to blame.

Kari called out a goodbye as we left her office and headed over to mine. I walked over to my desk and set down my coffee mug. With my back turned to Danny, I took in a few deep breaths. I could handle this. I could.

I dealt with over a hundred elementary-aged kids every day. What was one man? Why did he seem to shake my faltering confidence?

Realizing that I couldn't spend the whole time I was with him with my back turned, I slowly released my breath and faced him, forcing my signature vice principal smile. It hurt, sure, but it wasn't revealing. And right now, I was scared Danny was going to learn very quickly that he caused a reaction in me. A capability that I'd thought had shriveled up and died a long time ago. When I was around Danny, I felt like a woman. And it had been a long time since I'd allowed myself to feel that way.

When my gaze met Danny's, his eyebrows rose. He studied me for a moment before he spoke. "You okay?"

The loud crashing I heard inside of my mind was all of

my confidence falling to the ground. I could tell he wasn't buying my smile. Oh, he was good.

Still, I couldn't stop. I needed to protect myself. "Sure. Yes. Of course." I pinched my lips together to stop myself from speaking more. People who were fine didn't repeat themselves incessantly. "Yes, I'm fine." I finished with an air of accomplishment, like I'd somehow stuck the landing.

He chuckled and straightened. I couldn't help but notice how much taller he was than me. And I couldn't help my gaze from drifting over his broad shoulders, tapered waist...

Heat permeated my cheeks once more.

I needed to see a shrink.

"Come on, I'll bring you to meet Patty," I said as I turned and half walked, half ran from my office. I wasn't sure he was following me, but at this point, I didn't care. Even though part of me was excited that he was here—and not a figment of my imagination—the emotion I was feeling most explicitly was dread. Dread that my new start was going to be confused by his presence. And dread that, with him around, I was only going to become more and more aware of how much of a fool I was to even allow myself to be attracted to him.

There were single, perky, and young teachers here for him to flirt with. I was none of those things. Plus, I came with baggage. A whole lotta baggage. And from the looks of Danny, he probably rode in here on a motorcycle. He didn't have the capacity to deal with my baggage even if I wanted to fantasize that he could.

I let out my breath as we approached Patty's room. I could hear Bella's voice carry from the open door. I'd wanted this to be an in-and-out situation.

"The room is here," I said, waving my arm. And then I felt like an airport signaler so I dropped my arms and forced a smile.

Danny was watching me with this twinkle in his eye that I couldn't quite read. His lips were tipped up into a half smile as if he were enjoying a private joke. It infuriated me to watch him stand there, studying me.

Was he laughing at me? Had I said something wrong? Done something wrong?

Not wanting to go down a rabbit hole that I was pretty sure I wouldn't get out of, I pushed all worry from my mind and headed into Patty's room. After a short introduction, I excused myself and hurried back into the hallway. Bella called a quick goodbye as I left, and I waved my hand in her direction. I loved my daughter, but right now, I needed to focus on leaving. I was sure if I stayed in Danny's presence for much longer, I was going to self-destruct.

I needed to get back to my office and hide until I no longer felt this way.

I pulled open the office door, and as I headed past Cassidy's desk, she called after me. Not wanting to be rude, I stopped and slowly turned to face her.

"What did you say?" I asked. I honestly hadn't heard

her. I'd been so focused on getting to my office and shutting the door that her question had not even entered my brain.

"Who was that?" she asked. Her goofy smile and wiggle of her eyebrows turned my stomach. Not because she thought he was attractive—because he was. No, it was because her reaction only solidified what I already knew. That the women of Magnolia Elementary were going to be *very* interested in the new sub, which meant I was a fool for even allowing myself to be attracted to him.

"Just the new sub for Patty's class," I said as I inched closer to my office.

"Ah." Cassidy's gaze drifted back to the hallway. I moved to take her distraction as my opening to disappear, but stopped when she glanced back at me. "Is he single?"

I didn't want to answer that question. I really didn't. As soon as I told Cassidy, it would become school-wide knowledge. But, if I was sure I could never have something with him, why would I stop someone else?

"I'm not sure, but I think so," I said. My tongue felt like molasses in my mouth as I spoke.

I hated the glint of excitement that shone in Cassidy's gaze and the hinted smile that grew on her lips. She was plotting something already, and as much as I loved this girl, a pang of jealousy shot through my chest.

I hated that feeling.

"I should get back," I said as I nodded toward my office, but Cassidy was no longer paying attention to me.

Instead, she had her phone out, and from the way her fingers were moving, she was texting someone.

I disappeared into my office, the feeling of defeat surrounding me. I flopped down into my chair and sighed. I was an idiot and naive. Did I really think that my first foray into the dating world would be smooth and heartbreak-free?

Of course, it wasn't going to be that way. I was going to fall hard for men who could never fall for me. And honestly, as I thought about it, I began to feel relief. There was no time like the present to get over my ex-husband and have my heart broken by a new and unattainable man.

If I was going to have to suffer through both situations, I might as well do them at the same time.

Then, I could finally move on.

Then, I just might find my happiness.

In terms of my dating life, Craig was gone, and Danny was going to follow. And that determination made me feel better.

Well, almost.

VICTORIA

I was in a meeting, yet again.

Today had been dragging, and as much as I was trying to pay attention to Sawyer, I was losing interest. He was listing off places I needed to be that evening to make an appearance. Apparently, I was handing out doughnuts at the Star Dollar Bakery at five and then hosting a bowl-a-thon at Pete's Billiards at seven.

I was going to have half an hour for dinner at the diner, where I was expected to take pictures and shake hands.

My evening was booked solid.

And that thought weighed on my shoulders to the point that I felt as if it was going to crush me flat.

"Do we need to go over the plan?" Sawyer asked me.

I blinked a few times, bringing me back to the present, and nodded. "No. I got it."

Sawyer looked as if he didn't believe me, but thankfully he didn't push further. Instead, he shifted his focus back to Tracy, who was sitting next to him, taking notes. Their conversation was low as if they didn't want to bother me with details, so I stood and made my way from the conference room.

Brooke was sitting at her desk when I passed by. She was my assistant and receptionist here at city hall. She was talking on the phone, and when she saw me, she waved.

I nodded as I paused to pick up the stack of messages that she'd collected for me. I grabbed them and held them up. Brooke nodded a response.

With the messages in hand, I headed toward my office and shut the door behind me. After dropping the messages onto my desk, I collapsed in my chair and sighed. The last few days had been stressful. Dad was concerned about my reelection, so he'd decided against taking a trip to Montreal so that he could stay in the house with me.

Danny took up residence in the basement, which was nice—after all, he took some of the heat off of me—but he spent most of his time hiding away. So my normally quiet life had gotten louder and nosier.

Mom had attempted to bring up my dating life at dinner the night before, but I shut the conversation down before it could grow legs. There was no way I wanted to discuss my nonexistent love life with my parents. Besides the fact that my parents would feel the need to vet everyone I was interested in, I wasn't ready to prove to my parents just how much of a loser I was in the love department.

I could succeed at my job, but my heart was another story.

Feeling ridiculous for having dwelled on that minute-long conversation for as long as I had, I cleared my throat and mind as I sat up and stared down at my messages. I shouldn't be focusing on my family or my reelection. Right now, my attention needed to be on the work I needed to do as mayor.

Everything else was going to have to wait.

————

Too bad ignoring things didn't make them go away. Four o'clock rolled around, and even though I'd finished making calls and most of the work I needed to do, my looming personal to-do list was still hanging over me as I grabbed my jacket and slipped it on.

I wanted to go home, crawl into the bathtub, and stay there until I shriveled up like a prune. But, as Sawyer's fourth text in the last ten minutes caused my phone to buzz, I was nowhere near relaxing.

I needed to be at Star Dollar Bakery in twenty minutes or I was going to be late.

I closed my eyes for a moment and stilled my mind. My fingers were curled around the handle of my brief-case, and I was ready to go. I just needed to prep myself. For the next few hours, I needed to be approachable

Victoria. I needed to be friendly mayor Victoria. I needed to push out all of the stress that was weighing me down and pretend that Holts never have issues. That the mayor was as put together as her constituents could want.

After a mental pep talk, I headed out of my office, waving at Brooke as I passed by. I set my briefcase in the back seat and climbed in behind the wheel.

It took about fifteen minutes to get to Star Dollar Bakery. When I pulled up, I saw that a table had been set up, and Mom was busy laying out a tablecloth on top of it.

I took in a sharp breath as I instantly located Dad. He was standing off to the side, talking to Sawyer.

Suddenly, the thing that had been set up for *me* had turned into something for *them*. It was no longer about me meeting with the citizens of Magnolia, it was now about my family's name and what that meant for the town.

Great.

I pulled into the back parking lot and turned off the engine. I pulled my keys from the ignition and opened the door. Thankfully, no one seemed to notice that I'd arrived, which allowed me to linger in the background as they set up. Dad was talking to Sawyer about the flow of traffic, and Mom was directing Janae where to set up the boxes behind the table so they would be easy to access during peak time.

I leaned against the outside of the building and just watched the conversion as it played out in front of me. I was irritated that they were here, controlling the situation, but I also didn't want to step in and shift their focus from their tasks to me.

"Busy at work, I see," Danny's voice spoke near my ear, and I startled, turning to see him standing inches from me with a grin on his lips and a teasing glint in his gaze.

I glared at him and emphasized my irritation with a quick jab of my elbow. "Creeper much?" I asked, as I turned back to the scene I'd been watching before he so rudely interrupted me. "What are you doing here, anyway? I figured you'd be halfway to Bora-Bora by now."

Mom had convinced him to go to the elementary school to check out the substitute teaching job. He'd agreed but mumbled, *I need to get out of here,* as he'd stalked out of the house this morning. When I hadn't gotten a panicked call from Mom demanding that I tell her where Danny went, I'd figured he'd decided to stay. Which was strange for my brother.

When Danny didn't respond right away, I turned to see that his smile had faded, and he looked serious as he studied Mom and Dad.

"Danny?" I asked as I dipped down to catch his attention.

He didn't look down at me right away. His gaze lingered on the scene in front of us, and then he sighed and focused on me. "I don't know. I just figured sticking around might be fun."

I furrowed my brow. Danny had never said *Magnolia* and *fun* in the same sentence before. He'd spent his life trying to get away from this place, not stick around.

Something must have happened at the school to change his mind.

And then realization dawned on me. He'd met someone. And she must be good to cause this wanderer to want to set down roots. This intrigued me.

"What?" Danny asked. He looked shy, which was strange for my sickeningly confident brother.

"Who is she?" I demanded, as I turned to face him head-on.

Danny's jaw dropped, and he took a step back. "I don't know what you are talking about." He raised his hands as if that were going to protect him from my questions.

It wasn't. I was going to find out which of the Magnolia ladies had caught his attention.

"Who is she?" I asked again, this time taking advantage of an opening and jamming my finger into his ribs.

He yelped and hunched over. He kept his elbows tucked in close as he waved away my hands. "Will you stop that? It's not going to look good for the mayor to be abusing her sibling."

"If you tell me who she is, I'll stop," I said as I readied my finger and scanned him, looking for another opening.

I dove in, but he beat me to it and pushed my hand away. I laughed as I dodged his push and moved to poke him again. "Why won't you tell me who she is?"

Danny must have had enough of my pokes because, a moment later, he had his arms wrapped around my whole body, pinning my arms to my sides and effectively cutting off my ability to move.

"There isn't a girl," he said.

I stilled and then turned around to face him. I'd always thought he was into women, but maybe I was wrong. Danny let me go, and after one look at me, he shook his head. "It's not that either."

I parted my lips but then shrugged. "You never know."

Danny held up his hand. "No, I know. And that is not it."

I crossed my arm over my chest, resting my elbow on my hand as I drummed my chin with my fingers. "So you've just fallen in love with Magnolia all of a sudden?" Then I forced a sappy expression. "You missed your sister that much." I lunged forward with both arms open.

He jumped back and swatted me away. "Actually, I think you're right. I think a trip to Bora-Bora is just what I need." He moved to walk away, but I scrambled to grab ahold of his arm and pull him back.

"I'm just joking. Please stay." When he didn't move, I leaned closer. "I need your help dealing with crazy *a* and crazy *b*." I tossed my head in the direction of our parents.

Danny glanced down at me and then chuckled. "Alright, you convinced me," he said as he pulled me into a big bear hug. After a moment, he reached up and tousled my hair, a typical Danny move for when things got a little too emotional.

I pulled away from him and smacked his hand from my head. He laughed and then shoved his hands into his pockets. He whistled as he walked away from me and over to where Mom was arranging and then rearranging the doughnuts on the table.

I took a moment to straighten my now tousled hair. I made sure that my shirt was tucked into my pencil skirt, and I smiled and frowned as a way to warm up my facial muscles.

Now that I was prepped, I put on my Mayor Holt demeanor and marched over to where Sawyer and Dad were talking. They both greeted me but didn't move to let me into the conversation. Instead, I found myself just standing off to the side and listening to their plans. Apparently, Dad had got the Newport News to come over and do a small exposé on me and my reelection. I swallowed my nerves as I stared at Dad.

It was frustrating that he'd done this without asking me. I knew it was a good thing, but it still bothered me that the first person he told was Sawyer and not his daughter who was going to be on the screen.

But it was already planned, and if I sent the press away now, I'd look like I was trying to hide something. Sawyer had informed me that the town already had a negative view of my personality. That at times I came across as harsh.

So no matter how much I hated the fact that Dad went behind my back and arranged this news story, I was going to use the exposure to my advantage and show Magnolia how personable I could be.

As the night progressed, people began to show up. I stood at the table, handing out doughnuts. People seemed comfortable enough to linger around the table and lawn of the Star Dollar Bakery. I also took it as a good sign that residents of Magnolia were smiling and speaking with me for longer than a few seconds.

I just might be able to win over the voters I needed to win this election once more.

Danny was hanging out with me by the table. He took over handing out doughnuts while I did my short interview with the couple of reporters that showed up, and when I got back to the table, he had a mischievous look in his eye. Like he wanted to ask me a question but wasn't sure how to do it.

It intrigued me. Danny was anything but mysterious.

He was a wear his heart on his sleeve kind of guy.

"What's up?" I asked as I pulled out a cinnamon twist doughnut and began pulling off chunks to slip into my mouth. There was a lull in people, and I was starving. I'd forgotten lunch, and with my schedule jam-packed with events tonight, I knew dinner was a far-off reality.

Danny pulled out a jelly-filled doughnut and took a bite. "Nothing," he said through the food.

I shook my head. "Nope. Not buying it. You look like you've been up to something." I took another bite of the doughnut. "Did something happen at the school today?" I knew sending my good-looking brother into the clutches of the single elementary school teachers might have been a mistake. But, from the look on Danny's face, he didn't feel the same.

He swallowed his food. "What do you know about the vice principal?" he asked slowly.

"Vice principal?" I asked. And then realization dawned on me. "You mean Shari?"

Danny nodded. "Yeah. Shari."

I furrowed my brow. Why did he want to know about Shari? And how was it that he didn't recognize her? We'd all grown up together. "She's—"

"Sorry I'm late. I couldn't get Tag out of his room." Shari's out-of-breath voice caused me to turn. Her hair was windblown and her cheeks were red. She had one hand wrapped around Bella's, and she was half dragging her across the grass. Tag was lingering behind her, and from what I could see of his expression, he was not excited to be here. "I…"

I glanced up to see that she was staring just to the left of where I stood. Her eyes were wide, and her lips were parted as if she had more to say, but her words had left her mind and her mouth. I could tell something was bothering her, so I peeked over my shoulder to see the very familiar half smile of my brother. The one he used when he was flirting with his next fling.

Ugh.

This was not a good sign.

"It's fine. I'm just happy you made it," I said as I turned my attention to Bella, who was standing next to the table, eyeing all the doughnuts. "Do you want this one?" I asked, pointing to a chocolate-glazed doughnut with sprinkles.

Bella nodded shyly, and I pulled a piece of tissue paper

from the box next to me and fished out the doughnut. As I handed it to her, Shari and Danny still hadn't spoken a word. In fact, I was fairly certain that Shari was having a brain aneurysm.

Part of me didn't want to burst the bubble of whatever was playing out in front of me. But the other half of me felt like the pickle in the middle, and I was ready to get this conversation over with.

"Danny says he's working at the school with you," I said as I fiddled with my half-eaten doughnut. I was exhausted and no longer hungry, but my hands needed something to do.

"Do you know Danny?" Shari asked as she flicked her finger between the two of us.

I raised my eyebrows as I studied her, and then a moment later, recognition dawned on her. A mixture of fear and frustration passed through her gaze. "Oh my gosh," she whispered as her cheeks reddened. "I'm such an idiot."

Well, this exchange had only piqued my interest more. Something had happened between Danny and Shari, and from the embarrassed expression on Shari's face, it was something juicy. It would give me a distraction from the chaos that was my life and this reelection.

And right now, a distraction was what I needed.

9

SHARI

I was an idiot. A huge, colossal idiot.

Danny was Daniel Holt. As in the Holt family. As in Victoria's younger brother.

And I'd allowed myself to fantasize about him on numerous occasions.

I shook my head as I attempted to ground myself in the present. Thank goodness I hadn't allowed anything else to happen. If my crush hadn't gone away after he decided to work at my school, discovering who his family was sure did the trick.

At least, that was what I was trying to convince myself of as I glanced over at him. He was smiling at me again. Why did he have to look so good?

I was in trouble.

"Are we too late?" Maggie's voice pulled me from my thoughts. Grateful for the backup and distraction, I whipped my gaze over to see her walking up to the table.

She was holding hands with Archer, and her cheeks were rosy from the cool evening air.

"Nope," Victoria said as she reached for some tissue paper. "I've got plenty left."

Maggie nodded, and after she and Archer picked their doughnuts, they lingered by the table that I couldn't seem to walk away from. It was as if I were rooted to the spot. My mind was so muddled that making any decisions for myself didn't seem within my capability.

"You feeling okay?" Maggie asked as she dipped down to catch my gaze. Her smile was genuine, and it felt like the lifeline I needed right now.

"Yep. Mmhmm." I focused on eating my doughnut and turned my attention to scout out where Bella had disappeared to. Tag was easy to spot. After getting his doughnut from Victoria, he'd scurried over to a nearby tree where he plopped down and disappeared into whatever game he was playing on his Game Boy.

At least with him, I didn't fear losing him in the physical way. Just in the mental and emotional way.

Ugh. My life was a hot mess right now.

"Have you met my brother?" Victoria asked Maggie.

Intrigued with their conversation, I leaned in closer to listen.

"I don't think so," Maggie said. From the corner of my eye, I saw her reach across the table and shake Danny's hand. "But it's nice to meet you."

"You too," Danny said. His smile spread across his lips

once more, and despite my best efforts, my knees weakened again.

Stupid. Stupid knees.

Yet, no matter how much I yelled at my body parts to stop reacting to Danny, they refused to listen. My lips tipped up into a smile, and my entire body leaned closer to where Danny stood. They didn't care that I'd known Danny growing up. Or that I was a middle-aged divorcée with two kids, and he was a twenty-something guy with more girls on speed dial than I had takeout menus in my kitchen drawer.

We weren't even on the same playing field, and yet my body didn't care, no matter how much my mind tried to tell it otherwise.

Not wanting to stand around and feel ridiculous anymore, I crumpled up the rest of my doughnut in the tissue and threw it into the garbage. I gave everyone at the table a quick nod before excusing myself and heading over to where Bella was doing cartwheels with Chasity, a girl from her class at school.

I needed to get out of here before I did something more to embarrass myself. Right now, the only thing that seemed somewhat palatable was getting home and taking a bath. I would lick my wounds and vow never to go out to a club or look at a man again.

If my first foray back into the dating world turned out this way, then I was an idiot to attempt it again.

Bella wasn't happy to leave, and Serenity, Chasity's mom, offered to bring her home. I wasn't in the mood to fight Bella, so I agreed out of sheer desire to get the heck out of here. Tag was already at the car when I turned to focus my attention on him. He had his earbuds in, and his dark hair fell over his forehead as he kept his attention on his phone.

Relieved that I was that much closer to getting out of here, I headed in his direction. I was so focused on leaving that I didn't have enough time to stop when someone stepped in front of me. I braced myself as I rammed into his broad chest. I raised my hands in an effort to protect myself, but that resulted in my fingers sprawled across his muscles and the warmth of his body radiating across my skin.

I didn't have to look up to realize who this was. All I had to do was smell his cologne and hear his chuckle.

Danny.

"You're on a mission," he said softly. His hands had found their way to my upper arms, and he held them for a moment before he gave them a quick squeeze and stepped back.

I didn't want to look up, but there was no way I could stop myself. As soon as my gaze met his and I took in the warmth that emanated from his warm brown eyes, I knew that I was in trouble. Deep, sticky trouble.

"I need to get home," I said quickly as I sidestepped him.

He chuckled and moved to stand in front of me once more. "Are you sure that's it?"

I nodded—probably a bit too fervently—as I kept my

gaze focused on my car. "Of course that's it. What else would there be?"

Danny dipped down in an effort to meet my gaze, but I didn't move to acknowledge him. I was weak. I was broken. And I was disappointed in myself. One nice look from a handsome man, and suddenly I didn't know who I was or where I was going. I should be stronger. I needed to be stronger.

"Nothing," he said quietly. Even in his silence, I could tell something was bothering him. "It's just that you seem withdrawn." He cleared his throat. "Does this have anything to do with who I am?"

His direct question threw me off guard, and I glanced up at him.

He pursed his lips and nodded. "It does," he whispered.

"Listen, I had no idea that you were Victoria's brother. You look...different." Just as those words left my lips, I wanted to take them back. I didn't want him to have that kind of window into my soul.

"And you're disappointed now that you know?" His tone was so earnest that I couldn't help but focus on him. He looked disappointed as he stared down at me.

How could he be so open? Didn't he know that I was just ending my marriage? That I was damaged goods? That I came with not only two kids but stretch marks and a mom bod? He could have anyone on the island, and yet he was standing in front of me.

Because he pities you. The words entered my mind before I had time to police them. But the more I tried to understand his niceness to me or why he was standing here in the parking lot, talking to me instead of someone else—the more I began to realize that he pitied me.

That was all.

It wasn't that he was interested in me. Or that he had any of the same thoughts that I did. He just saw a broken, divorced woman, and he took pity on me.

And I was the idiot who'd allowed myself to have deeper feelings for him.

"I should go," I said quickly as I ducked my head and moved to walk around him and over to my van.

"Wait." His hand surrounded mine, halting my retreat.

I paused as my gaze slipped down to our hands. A rush of emotions exploded from my hand, up my arm, and into my chest. I sucked in my breath. I felt like I'd been hit by a semi. I hadn't had these kinds of responses in a long time. It was so foreign. So new.

And even though I didn't want to admit it, it felt good.

So good.

Too scared to allow myself to enjoy the touch of a man again, I pulled my hand away quickly. I didn't want to encourage him even though my entire body told me to lean in, and the desire to have him wrap his arms around me grew strong.

I folded my arms and turned my attention to him. With my hands safely tucked away, there were no more chances for us to accidentally touch. I would stay in my space, and he would stay in his. "Yes?" I asked, hoping that he wouldn't push me out of my comfort zone more than he already had.

I was so close to breaking, and I couldn't do that right now. Not when I was barely hanging on.

He paused as he studied me. His eyes were narrowed as if he were trying to read me. I offered him a weak smile and hoped it came across as relaxed.

"Can I take you out for dinner sometime?"

All of my breath left my body in one whoosh. I blinked a few times as I stared at him. Was he serious? Had he just asked me out on a…date?

"I…um…" I pursed my lips as I studied him.

He let out a nervous chuckle as he raised his hands. "Not like that. As friends. Colleagues even." He tucked his hands into his front pockets and raised his shoulders as if he were trying to seem relaxed.

It was adorable that he seemed as nervous as I felt. And then I pushed that thought from my mind. Of course, he wasn't nervous like I was. He was a player, and I was a middle-aged mom. To think that he had any desire for me was ridiculous.

"Let me think about it," I said quickly. I didn't want to say yes, and I also didn't want to stand here debating whether I should say no. So being elusive felt like the right move.

He perked up at my response. It seemed as if he'd been waiting for me to say no. And I almost felt bad for leading him on. Even if I wanted to, I couldn't go out to dinner with a guy younger than me. And there was no way I could go on a date with Victoria's brother.

None of these situations would end happily. And I was tired of being sad.

"Perfect," he said with a subtle wink.

I hated the fact that my heart rate picked up, and I hated that, for a moment, I wished I had just said yes.

That I could allow myself to have fun for once.

The sound of a car horn blaring drew my attention, and through the windshield of my van, I saw Tag wave his hand at me. With one of the reasons why I couldn't just throw caution to the wind and enjoy myself currently staring at me, I nodded and threw Danny an apologetic smile.

"I gotta go," I said.

Danny looked embarrassed as he stepped to the side. "Oh, right. Sorry."

I shrugged as I passed by him. And then, without thinking, I glanced at him over my shoulder to see him watching me. There was a hint of desire on his expression that got my heart rate galloping again.

Could it be possible that he was attracted to me like I wanted him to be? Like no man had been in a long time?

Did I dare hope?

"I'll see you at the school tomorrow?" he called after me.

I nodded and waved in his direction as I climbed into the driver's seat and started my van. Thankfully, he remained rooted to the ground as I drove off. I was struggling with self-control when he wasn't around, and it was ten times worse when he was standing next to me, shooting his sexy half smile in my direction.

He was so carefree. It caused a longing inside of my heart that I hadn't felt in a long time. The desire to be me mixed with the reality of my situation and waged a war inside of me. I wanted to be free, but I wanted to do what was right for my family.

Why couldn't both things happen at once? And why couldn't I feel good about the decision that I needed to make either way?

Was I always going to have to give up something in the pursuit of something else? Was I ever just going to be happy? That word seemed so far from my grasp that I felt like an idiot for even thinking it.

I should have been satisfied with where I was. Craig was gone, and I didn't have the weight of his bad decisions hanging onto me and dragging me down. Why couldn't I just let things lie?

Why did I have to want Danny like I did?

I groaned as I came to a stop at a red light and rested my forehead on my hand. I took in a few deep breaths in an effort to ground myself in the present.

I was ridiculous. There was no way around it. I should know better than to assume I could be different. If I wanted to heal from the trauma that came from being married to Craig, then I needed to take time to just be me. Not whatever I was with Danny.

Trying to let someone into my life just resulted in a big giant mess.

Tag didn't say anything as I drove home, which I was grateful for. I needed time to think, to convince myself that I really didn't want to go to dinner with Danny, that I was okay with my life just consisting of me and my kids. I didn't need a man—I knew that. But that didn't mean I didn't want one.

For the first time in my life, I was beginning to wonder if I deserved a man. One who knew my worth. Who wanted to be with me in every sense of the word.

A man who could love me no matter what.

When I got to my room, I shut my door and threw myself on my bed. I buried my face in my comforter and let out a scream. This was not how I wanted to spend my evening. I'd been so confused after I saw Danny at school that I'd thought a night out with my kids would help clear my mind.

I'd been wrong.

I was more muddled and confused than ever.

10

VICTORIA

Exhaustion coated every muscle in my body as I climbed out of my car and slammed the driver's door behind me. I let out an exhale as I tipped my head back and closed my eyes to the stars that shone above me.

After the doughnut giveaway, I went with Sawyer over to Pete's Billiards for a *Bowl with the Mayor* extravaganza. A few people showed up—not as many as I'd hoped—but it was just the start of my reelection kickoff, I needed to keep my expectations grounded in reality.

Two headlights shone behind me, and I turned to squint in their direction. Mom and Dad had tagged along. Even though that irritated me to no end, I'd tried to hide my frustration with a cheek-sore smile the whole night.

Right now, the last thing I wanted was to have an in-depth discussion with my father about why I couldn't pack a small-town bowling alley. I didn't need a lecture on how I needed to be more open and inviting. I didn't need him to tell me how he would do it better.

I didn't need him to tell me how much I'd failed him.

I was already feeling like a failure. I didn't need it to be reiterated by the man who raised me. At least, not right now.

I tightened my grip on my purse and headed into the house. I didn't wait for them to get out of their car. Instead, I shut the back door and hurriedly kicked off my shoes. With my heels in my hand, I sprinted across the marble floor and up the stairs to my room. Even though my stomach was rumbling from hunger, there was no way I was going to chance an interaction with my parents.

I was going to hide out in my room until the coming of Christ if that meant I wasn't going to have to face them and their disappointment.

With my bedroom door shut, I tossed my purse onto my bed and my shoes in the direction of my closet. I slipped out of my clothes and into my pajamas. I could hear Mom and Dad's muffled voices downstairs, and I tried to swallow the acid that had risen up in my throat.

It was only a matter of minutes before they made their way upstairs and into my room. It was only a matter of minutes before I had to sit there while they stared down at me in disappointment.

My life sucked.

I was a grown woman, but that didn't seem to matter to them. I was forever going to be their puppet. Jumping when they said to jump. Sitting when they commanded I sit. I was relegated to the same status as Blossom, our family dog growing up.

Where was Danny? I was ready for him to take some of the heat off of me.

After I crawled under my covers, I located my phone in my purse and pulled it out. I clicked on our text chain and opened it.

Me: Where are you? I could use some backup.

Thankfully, it didn't take Danny long to respond.

Danny: Who is this?

I rolled my eyes and sent a *har har*.

Me: I mean it. I could use my brother.

Those words never felt truer as I sat in my bed like a little girl waiting for her parents to discover that she broke a dish. I hated feeling like this. I hated feeling out of control. I wanted to be seen as the responsible woman I'd become. Not the feeble woman I felt like I would always be to my parents.

Danny: Rolling in right now. I grabbed some pizza. Want me to bring you a slice?

My mouth watered at the thought of cheese, sauce, and warm bread. All of the ingredients that always managed to make my crappy days seem better.

Me: Yes please.

He responded with a thumbs-up. Hoping he would have a straight shot from the kitchen to my bedroom without any interruptions, I flopped back into my pillows and located my remote. After I found some sappy romantic movie, I settled back and let out my breath.

I could do this. I could. Reelection couldn't be that hard. After all, I was a Magnolia resident through and through. Being mayor once had to count for something. Dad wasn't giving me enough credit, and it was really starting to bug me.

Ten minutes ticked by and Danny still hadn't appeared. I sighed as I flung off my comforter and dropped my feet to the ground. I padded over to my door and cracked it, leaning in to hear what was happening downstairs.

Dad was talking, and I waited for a break in what he was saying so I could assess if Danny was with them.

"Yep, I know," Danny's voice carried upstairs.

Great. They had cornered him.

Mom said something, but I couldn't quite make it out. But I knew the tone in her voice. She was desperate and unhappy. No doubt she was all in a tizzy because of Danny's life choices and the fact that he was still single.

I used to think my parents wanted us to get married because they wanted us to be happy and not lonely. But that was back when I thought my parents cared about our happiness. Now I was realizing that Mom and Dad wanted connections. They wanted us to marry who they wanted us to marry.

And they wanted us to marry people who would help elevate our family name. That was it.

A bad taste grew in my mouth, so I shut my door and hurried back over to my bed. If Danny was taking the heat, I would let him. I needed a break. After all, he'd been gone for so long that he'd had a reprieve from their constant nagging. It was my turn to take a breather before they started in on me again.

By the time Danny made it to my room, he looked frazzled. His hair was tousled, and he had a fiery look in his eye as he balanced the pizza box on his arm and used the hand that was holding a six-pack of beer to shut the door. Once he'd shut out the rest of the house, he let out a long groan.

"Thanks for that," he said as he shot daggers in my direction.

I couldn't help but laugh. Partly because it was funny that it wasn't me. And partly because just hearing the stress in his voice amplified my own, and I needed a way to release that tension.

I knew the pain that was written across his face. It was as acute as the pain that resided inside of me—despite my efforts to pretend that I didn't care.

"Come on over here," I said as I patted the empty side of my bed. "We can commiserate together."

Danny let out a huff as he paused and stared me down. "That was unfair," he said as his shoulders slumped and he made his way over.

I pushed out my bottom lip and nodded. "I know."

He set the pizza down on my legs and the beer down on the nightstand and then kicked off his shoes. "I hadn't even gotten into the house before Mom started talking about how she has a friend who has a friend who has a daughter." He paused as he pinched his lips and studied me. His eyes were wide as if that was all he needed to say for me to understand the gravity of what had happened to him.

Which was accurate. I understood his sentiments acutely.

"Ugh." I opened the box of pizza and pulled out a slice. Even though it was colder now than I was sure it had been when he got home, I didn't care. I was ravenous and ready to eat anything that came my way.

Danny plopped down next to me and sighed. "It's like she seems to think I can't get a girlfriend on my own." He turned to face me. "I mean, come on. I have girls throwing themselves at me."

I was mid chew, but his words made me inhale and caused little bits of crumbs to fly to the back of my throat. I swallowed what was in my mouth as tears filled my eyes. Once my mouth was clear, I started coughing and hacking until the tickle in my throat died down.

When I could finally focus on something, I glanced over to see Danny eating his pizza while he watched me. His eyebrows were raised, and his chin moved up and down. I glared at him as I pulled his open beer from his hands and took a swig.

"Thanks for *not* helping," I said after I'd taken a few drinks of the cold liquid.

Danny wrinkled his nose when I tried to hand it back to him. He waved his hand and reached over to grab a new can.

"You seemed to have it handled," he said as the clicking sound of the tab releasing filled the air.

"I could have died." I took a few more drinks before I returned to eating my pizza.

"But you didn't."

"But I could have." I gave him pointed look. "And then Mom and Dad's focus would be solely on you." I leaned in and let the gravity of my words fall around us.

Realization dawned on Danny, and he nodded. "Noted. Next time, I'll do more."

I chuckled as I leaned against my pillows. "That's all I wanted to hear."

"Glad I could help."

We were quiet for a moment before I remembered where we'd left off before I'd had my coughing fit. Danny thought he could date anyone, which made me wonder, was there someone in Magnolia he wanted to test this theory on?

"So who did Mom set you up with?"

Danny groaned as he popped the rest of his pizza crust into his mouth. "Do we have to talk about that?"

I shrugged. "I'm just wondering. I mean, how do you know she's terrible?"

He gave me a pointed look. "It's Mom's pick. It's going to be horrible."

"You never know…" I allowed my voice to trail off as I attempted the straightest face I could muster.

Danny just responded by rolling his eyes and grabbing another slice. "Eh, even *if* that were true, I'm not interested."

I snorted and fished out another slice as well. "Because there's someone else?"

I missed this. Bantering back and forth with my brother. Equally hating on our parents. It made me realize how lonely I'd been for the last year and a half that he'd been gone. I needed this. I needed people in my life to distract me from myself and allow me to just be...me.

I was rapidly beginning to forget who *me* even was.

When he didn't respond, I glanced over at him to see him thoughtfully studying the TV while he ate. His silence was deafening, and I began to realize there was someone. Someone that he didn't want to talk about.

Who could it be?

"There is?" I asked. I dropped my half-eaten slice into the pizza box, dusted off my hands, and turned to give him my undivided attention. "Do I know her?"

I studied his expression to see if anything changed. When he gave me an exasperated look, I realized that, yes, I did know her.

"Ooo, this is good." I rubbed my hands together. "You just got back so...is it someone at the school?"

He blinked a few times before he shook his head. His tell. He was lying.

"No," he said, but I knew otherwise.

"She works at the elementary school..." I tapped my chin. "Is it Cassidy?"

Danny shook his head. "No and no. It's not someone here in Magnolia, and it's nothing."

"So it's something," I replied as I leaned forward to

catch his gaze, which he seemed determined to keep from me.

"No. Am I not speaking English?" he asked as he took a swig of his beer. He finally met my gaze, and I could tell that he was lying. But that was strange. Why would he lie about a girl?

And then understanding washed over me. Because it was someone Mom and Dad wouldn't like.

"Who is she?" I asked in a hushed tone—I'd really meant it for myself. Who could he be interested in that he wasn't bragging about wanting him right now? Was it someone he couldn't have?

All this thinking just piqued my interest even more. I grabbed my pizza and settled back while I thought. There weren't a ton of single people in Magnolia. And there were even fewer that Danny would feel shy about admitting he liked.

"Is she old?"

His gaze whipped over to me. I leaned back from his reaction. It seemed a little out of place.

"She's old?" I asked again. How much older than him could she be? "Like, *old*, old?"

Danny scoffed and wrinkled his nose. "No."

His denial was an admission to there being a *she*. Now I was invested in finding out who *she* was.

"I mean, there's no one. So she's neither old nor young." His cheeks flushed as he pinched his lips together.

He knew that I knew. He was caught in a lie. And there was no way I was going to let this go.

"Oh this is good." I giggled as I started racking my brain for someone who was older than Danny and not someone my family would approve of.

"Just stop it." Danny closed the empty pizza box and tossed it onto the floor.

"Absolutely not. I need this distraction, and I'm not going to let you take this away from me." I pinched off a bit of the crust and slipped it into my mouth. "Is it Mrs. Danbury?" I whispered as I leaned in closer to him.

"Um, no," he said as he elbowed me. "I'm not interested in our old school librarian."

I giggled as I pulled away and sent him a shrug. "Hey, you never know when love will strike."

He gave me an annoyed look. "If I do fall in love with Mrs. Danbury, you should send me to the insane asylum because that's where I'd belong." He folded his arms across his chest and narrowed his eyes as he stared at the screen.

I snuggled deeper into my covers as I let out a sigh. It was fun picking on my brother. I'd be lying if I said I hadn't missed it. After all, he and I had always had each other through everything. Why did that have to end when we got older? Why couldn't we stay close?

"I'm happy you are home," I whispered as I grabbed a nearby fuzzy pillow and stroked it absentmindedly.

I could feel Danny turn to study me. Then he reached out and tousled my hair. I swatted his hand away with a growl.

"Are you sure it's not just because you want me to be the focus of Mom and Dad's craziness?"

I pretended to think on that before I gave him a serious look. "It's partly because of that, but mostly because I missed you." I hated being this vulnerable. It opened me up to the opportunity to be hurt. But right now, the fear of being alone was beginning to outweigh my fear of getting hurt.

And perhaps I was beginning to realize that no matter what I did, there was always the possibility of getting hurt. At least with someone by my side, I wasn't going to be alone.

Being alone sucked.

"Aww, who are you, and what did you do with Tori?" he asked.

I shrugged. "Age I guess."

Danny chuckled and then reached out to tousle my hair again. "I missed you too, big sis."

We shared a mutual smile before we settled back on the pillows. The movie that had been playing in the background now became our focus. I sighed, feeling the stress leave my body as my thoughts returned to Danny and what we'd talked about.

"I mean it, though. If you like her, I'm sure I will too." I tipped my face so I could see him. "Even if she's forty years older than you."

Suddenly, a pillow came into view as Danny smacked me with it. I yelped and grabbed the one from behind me and fired back.

"I appreciate your support," Danny said as he twisted and slipped off the bed to avoid my second blow.

I laughed as I leapt up and moved to follow him. "Anything I can do for my lovestruck baby brother."

Our pillow fight didn't last long. After a few minutes, we were both tired and sweating. It was nothing like we used to do. Age seemed to be catching up with us.

Danny stood and scrubbed his face. I picked up our empty cans and the pizza box and handed them over to him. He took them and leaned forward to give me a quick kiss on the top of my head.

"I've gotta go to bed. I have to be an adult tomorrow and go to work."

I yawned and nodded. "Same."

He pulled back and gave me a quick once-over. "You're going to be okay?"

I knew he could tell that I wasn't okay, but I really didn't want his pity. Not right now at least. "I'll be fine."

"You sure?"

I nodded again.

He paused before turning to leave. "I'll always be here," he said over his shoulder.

I laughed and held the door as I watched him walk out to the hallway. "I know."

He gave me a smile, and I waved as I shut the door on his retreating frame.

Now alone, I took a deep breath. That was the break that I'd needed. I loved that for a moment I could focus on something other than my reelection or the stress my parents put on me.

But, just like every vacation from my problems, once

the moment was over, reality came crashing down, leaving me wanting more than before. I knew what happiness felt like, so when it was gone, the absence was that much more potent.

I knew what I wanted for the first time in my life. And I was beginning to realize that what I had wasn't what I wanted.

Yet, no matter how much I wanted things to change, they never did.

And I knew that was partly because I didn't know how to make the change or what that change would look like.

I didn't know if I had the strength to see it through. Or who I would be after the change took place.

I wasn't sure I was ready for an overhaul no matter how much I may want it.

The fear was real. So real that it scared me.

And I hated feeling scared.

11

SHARI

My stomach was in knots. All night and all morning. My entire body felt on edge as I got ready and drove to school. As much as I was trying to keep my mind off Danny and the way he spoke to me yesterday, it was proving impossible.

Every time someone walked by the office or my phone rang, my entire body tensed in anticipation. Anticipation that Danny would come walking into my office with sexy swagger and his half smile that he'd direct at me.

Just thinking of him got my heart pounding, and my entire body flushed with warmth. I wanted to see him again. I wanted to make sure that what had transpired between us had been real. That I hadn't just made up the way he looked at me or the way I felt when he was around.

I wanted to feel that way again.

It was exciting and exhilarating. And for a moment in

my life, I wanted to be selfish and experience it again. I wanted to be Shari the woman once more. Apparently, she wasn't as dead as I'd once thought. With the way I was feeling, she was very much alive and knocking at the door to be let out.

Three solid knocks on my office door caused me to jump and whip my gaze up. I must have looked crazed because Cassidy stepped back with a confused expression. "You okay?" she asked.

Feeling like an idiot, I released the breath that I'd been holding and nodded. "Yeah, why?" Did I sound normal? Did I sound relaxed? Or did I sound just as discombobulated as I felt?

From the unconvinced look on Cassidy's face, I knew the answer. I sounded completely discombobulated.

Great.

I cleared my throat and stood. I straightened my suit coat and offered her a smile. "What's up?"

I hadn't noticed that she was holding a stack of papers to her chest until she stepped into my room and handed then over. "I just have a few things for you to look over before I give them to Kari for her signature."

"Oh?" I asked as I took the stack and glanced at the top paper. "Oh, sports stuff."

She nodded and then moved to lean against my desk. "What's with you and Daniel?"

My entire body tensed as I moved to set the papers down. The last thing I needed was to randomly drop them on the floor and pique her already heightened interest in me. "Daniel? Who's Daniel?" I winced at my strained voice. What was wrong with me?

Apparently, I was no longer an adult but a child on the playground trying to convince her friends that she didn't like a particular boy. I was beginning to spiral, and it was not a good look.

"Daniel Holt." Cassidy furrowed her brow. "I'm surprised you don't know. You're in a book club with his sister."

I let out my breath and allowed my shoulders to sag. I was tired of trying to pretend that I was okay when I so obviously was not. "I know who Daniel is," I said quietly. "What about him?"

Even though I slept a solid eight hours last night, all of this stress and pressure was getting to me, and I felt as if I could fall asleep on my floor if allowed. I was a mess. A colossal mess.

"Nothing. I just saw you talking to him in the parking lot last night." She leaned in. "What did you talk to him about?"

My cheeks heated at the mention of our conversation. I felt idiotic now that I knew people had seen us.

I shrugged and shook my head. "Nothing much. He was just asking me about school." I winced at the lie. I wasn't proud of it, but I didn't want to confess to Cassidy that he'd asked me to dinner. I knew how the gossip train worked in this school. Everyone would know my business by third period.

"He is hot," Cassidy said, revealing just how young she

was. Life seemed so simple for a twenty-four-year-old single woman.

For a moment, I allowed myself to feel jealous. She had freedom to like who she wanted. Not me. The dating pool for a single woman with two kids had to be the size of one of the toddler pools you can buy in the summertime. Small, shallow, and filled with all sorts of undesirable people.

Not something I even wanted to dip my toe into.

"Yeah," I said, not sure how to respond. Did I agree? Reject? How did one handle a situation like this?

Cassidy seemed lost in her thoughts before she perked up and turned to face me. "Do me a favor?"

If it meant her leaving my office and taking her talk of Danny with her, I was game for anything. "Sure."

"If you talk to him again, can you mention me?"

I almost choked on my tongue. I hadn't expected her to say that, so I had not prepped myself for a response. I knew she wanted me to be her bosom sister and exclaim that I'd help her out, but I literally could not say those words. They would not form on my tongue.

So I just offered her a strained smile and nodded.

That seemed satisfying enough as she gave me a wide grin and practically bounded from my office. Now alone, I collapsed back onto my chair and let out my breath. I closed my eyes as my anxiety reached an all-time high.

Maybe if I told Kari I was sick, she would let me go home and I could spend the rest of my life hiding under my covers. Away from Danny, away from Magnolia, and away from the brown envelope that was still sitting on my dresser, waiting for me to open it.

Why did my life just keep getting more and more complicated?

"You okay?"

Danny's deep voice caused me to groan.

I was trying to forget the man, and yet, I could literally hear him speak to me like he was right here in my office with me.

Then I yelped as I whipped open my eyes and straightened. My jerking motions caused my chair to roll back, and I almost lost my balance and landed flat on my bottom. My entire body felt as if it were on fire as I gripped my desk for support.

"Whoa," Danny said as he stepped inside and extended his hand. He looked as if he wanted to help but wasn't sure if he should.

Before he could touch me, I stood and let out a nervous laugh. "I'm okay. I'm okay. See?" I asked weakly as I brought my hands up to show I was fine.

He ran his gaze over me, and that only caused my heart rate to pick up more. "You sure?"

I nodded, pinching my lips together. "Yes." And then I furrowed my brow. "Did you need something? Is everything okay?"

My words seemed to relax Danny, and he slipped his hands into the front pockets of his Dockers. He was closer now, and he used my desk as a support for his hip as he leaned against it. "I'm good."

I waited for him to offer more, but when he didn't, I raised my eyebrows. "That's good." And then I glanced behind him and caught sight of Cassidy, who was watching us from her desk. Great. This was going to elicit another conversation that I didn't want to have. "Did you need anything?" I asked again as I returned my gaze to Danny.

"Yeah." He sucked in his breath as he reached out to fiddle with the pens in my pen cup. He looked nervous and it was adorable. "I was wondering if you wanted to eat lunch together."

My eyes widened as his question settled in my mind. Had he really just said the words that I thought he'd said? "Lunch?"

Danny moved his gaze from the pens and over to my face. His expression turned serious as he nodded. "Well, you didn't say yes to dinner, so I figured we could do something less intense and just eat lunch together." Then he leaned in, and the smell of his cologne wafted around me, intoxicating me. The smell mixed with the way his muscles rippled as he moved, making me sure that if he asked me to stand on my head, I would.

I was in trouble.

"I'm really busy," I offered. It was a lame excuse, but I needed him to leave before I agreed. What if I enjoyed being with him? Would I want to do it again? And where did I draw the line? Right now, it seemed wiser to just stay away than try to ration what I could or couldn't do when it came to him.

Staying away was the best option.

"Hey, Cassidy?" Danny leaned back so that he was in line with her.

She perked up and was out of her chair before I could shake my head in an effort to get her to stay where she was. She didn't take notice of my discomfort as she sprinted toward my office. "What's up?"

Danny waved in my direction. "When does Shari eat lunch?"

Cassidy looked confused but glanced up at the clock. "In about an hour, why?"

Danny shot me a grin and moved to leave my office. I hated how excited Cassidy seemed as he neared her. It was as if she thought that he was leaving with her. Which made me feel jealous...which in turn made me feel immature.

I was a mess.

Before I could protest, Danny was out of my office and across the room. I watched as he headed out into the hall and disappeared around the corner. I leaned back in my chair and let out my breath. Cassidy looked as if she wanted to talk, so I reached forward and grabbed my phone. She seemed to take the hint and gave me a smile as she returned to her desk.

After a few seconds of listening to the dial tone, I set my phone back down and rubbed my temples. What was an already stressful day had just been magnified ten times with Danny's invitation to lunch. The idea of taking a sick day seemed better and better the more I thought about sitting across from Danny. What would we even talk about? I didn't know much about him, and I was pretty sure the last things he wanted to talk about were my kids or my divorce.

How could I even be friends with this guy, much less... I shook my head. Friends. That was all we were going to be. If I allowed myself to imagine us being more, I was going to go crazy.

———

I wished I could say that I finally relaxed enough to get some work done, but that would have been a blatant lie. I spent the next hour staring at my computer screen and trying to force myself to answer an email, but my ability to form sentences had abandoned me. Everything had blended together into one mass, much like my thought process.

By the time Cassidy came into my office and announced that it was lunchtime, I was ready to get this whole lunch date over with so I could move on with my day and my life.

After grabbing my lunch from the fridge in the teacher's lounge, I found a table at the far end of the room and sat down. I winced when I remembered what I'd packed. Leftover spaghetti with a cucumber and an apple wasn't exactly what I wanted to sport in front of Danny. I didn't have a desire to hide the kind of mother I was, but I also wanted the blinders to stay on somewhat.

I'd rather him think I was more put together than I really was.

Thankfully, I ate my lunch when there were few teachers on lunch as well. I liked eating alone, and when there were others in the lounge, I always felt like I needed to talk to them. That hadn't always been a bad thing, but I hated how pleasantries always started with someone asking how you were.

I hated lying, but I also didn't want to dive into my current life status. So I just avoided the whole situation altogether and stayed to myself. But, when a figure filled the doorframe, and I glanced up to see Danny standing there, the fear that I'd made a big mistake washed over me.

Why was I here, and what was I doing? Did I think I could possibly be someone else? How could I have thought that this was a good idea?

I was losing my mind.

But I was trapped with nowhere to go. And when Danny located me and smiled as he walked over, I realized I was in trouble. I was actually doing this. A lunch date with a man. Regardless of how much I tried to tell myself that this wasn't a date, I couldn't help but feel as if it kind of was.

And that thought scared me more than I'd initially thought.

"I actually—"

But Danny grabbed my hand before I could finish what I was saying. He pulled me to my feet, grabbed my lunch box, and headed over to the fridge. His hand was firmly wrapped around mine as he deposited my lunch inside and shut the door. Then he dropped my hand and turned to face me. "Come on, I have a better idea."

My entire body felt numb. A better idea? What did that mean? Were we going to eat lunch?

Despite the warning bells that were sounding in my mind, I decided to allow myself to trust him. I followed after him as he led me through the lounge and out into the hallway.

Thankfully, we didn't run into anyone as he led me to the front doors and out into the parking lot. The warm sun shone down on me as the smell of leaves and early autumn surrounded me. I squinted as I hurried to catch up with Danny. He was headed to the back fields.

I was confused about what we were doing, but I was equally curious. Had he planned something? Was he taking me off to murder me?

It was both thrilling and terrifying at the same time.

Not because I really believed that he might murder me. More because he was taking charge of our afternoon together. It had been so long since a man had done anything for me. And for a moment, I felt wanted. I felt important. And it was amazing.

Danny led me over to one of the picnic tables that lined the field. I peeked around him to see that there was a small tablecloth spread over it. A thermos sat next to some covered white containers. As we got closer, I could make out what looked like cheese and meat.

"What is this?" I asked as Danny stopped at the table,

stepped to the side, and extended his hand toward the bench. I glanced up at him to see him smile and then tip his head in the direction he wanted me to go.

"It's lunch," he replied as I sat down. He hurried to sit across from me.

He unscrewed the lid of the thermos and, a moment later, handed me a steaming cup of hot chocolate. It smelled rich and creamy with just a hint of cinnamon. My mouth watered as I held the cup with both hands and then slowly tipped it so the warm liquid slid into my mouth.

I let out a tiny sigh as I set the cup down. Danny was watching me with an intrigued expression. I furrowed my brow, embarrassed that I'd let myself react that way to hot chocolate. But it was one of my favorite drinks.

"Taste good?" he asked, giving me a wink. He reached out and unsnapped the lid of one of the containers and opened it up, revealing some cubed cheese. I'd been right about the contents when he revealed the cut-up meats in the other container.

"Hot chocolate is nectar from the gods," I said as I watched him spear a chunk of cheese with a toothpick and hand it over. As I took it from him, my fingers brushed his, and a warm shot of electricity raced up my arm and exploded in my chest.

He chuckled as he speared some meat for himself. "Nectar from the gods?" he asked.

My cheeks flushed as I pinched my lips together. Was that corny? Was I wrong to have said that? Maybe I supposed to be mysterious and play hard to get.

How was I ever going to survive this new dating world?

Dating. Ha.

What Danny and I were doing wasn't dating. He was just being nice. If anything, he just wanted to be friends. I was the idiot who seemed to always want to add more meaning to his actions.

"I speak the truth," I replied. I might as well give up on the idea that I could, in some way, be mysterious. I wasn't suave, and I certainly wasn't cool enough to try to pretend otherwise. I was a mom with two kids who was trying to survive life. Anything other than that was a lie, and after what had happened with Craig, I was over living a life of deception.

Danny chuckled. "I like that about you." His voice was low and had an air of reverence to it that took me by surprise. And the way he was smiling up at me confused me.

Was he giving me a compliment? What did that mean? And how was I supposed to react? Thank him? Hit his arm and say something feminine?

Why was I overthinking everything?

He furrowed his brow before I could respond. He speared a piece of cheese and slipped it into his mouth. "Why do you look so bothered?" he asked.

I swallowed and shook my head, hoping that I could erase my anxiety and be the woman who knew how to handle this. Who was cool enough to flirt with Danny.

"I'm not," I whispered. Even though it was a blatant lie,

there was no way I wanted to explain to this man how broken I was.

Danny leaned back and folded his arms. My entire body flushed with embarrassment as I fiddled with the cheese on my toothpick. I was so nervous that eating seemed like a joke. My stomach was in knots, and hunger was the last thing on my mind. Even though I knew I was going to regret it later.

The silence between us was deafening. I wanted him to speak. I wanted him to tell me that he'd made a mistake and then walk away. I didn't want to get invested in a man that just might walk away from me when my secrets became exposed.

He was carefree and relaxed, and I was broken and tied down.

Why didn't he realize that?

Danny cleared his throat, and I brought my attention back to him. He leaned forward and met my gaze head-on. His lips tipped up into a smile, and he looked so at ease that I almost wanted to sprint away from him.

How could he be so confident right now?

"I like you, Shari," he said quietly.

Those four little words caught me off guard. I blinked a few times as they settled around me. I hadn't actually heard him say that...had I?

"I want to get to know you better. But I fear that if I push you, you'll just walk away." He leaned his elbow on the table and rested his chin on his palm. "But I also think that if I don't do the direct approach, you'll never pick up on my hints."

I was sure my eyes were as wide as saucers as I stared at him. Was he serious? Or was this a joke? My lips parted, but nothing came out. Instead, I just sat there, staring at him as he kept talking.

"I know what you are going to say. I'm too young for you. I'm a Holt. I'm not mature enough." He shifted on his seat. Was he nervous?

The reasons I had for us not being together had nothing to do with his age or his family—though when he mentioned those things, they did make me a tad nervous.

No. The reason I wanted to push him away had everything to do with me and my own baggage, not his.

"Geez, Danny," he said under his breath as he pinched his lips together and offered me a weak smile. "Listen to me, talking you out of giving me a chance."

I shook my head. That wasn't it. But he seemed to misinterpret my reaction because his expression fell as he pushed his hands through his hair.

"Yeah. That's what I figured. It was ridiculous for me to hope—"

"No!" I said so loud that it startled even me.

He snapped his head back and stared at me as if he expected me to attack him or something.

Embarrassment came over me, but I pushed it aside. Somehow, I was able to find the confidence that I was lacking and decided that if he could be vulnerable, so could I.

"I didn't mean the shake of my head as a no," I said quietly. Then I pinched my lips together. "I've just never had a guy be that interested in me."

It was nerve-racking to be that vulnerable with him, but when the words finally escaped my lips, I felt…better. Lighter.

"I don't believe that." His smile was wider this time, and I could tell that he meant what he was saying even if I had a hard time believing him.

"It's true."

Danny shook his head. "I'll have to take your word on that." Then he leaned forward again and gave me his knee-weakening smile. "What do you say? Give me a chance to take you out on a real date?"

I wanted to say no—I did. But I didn't have the strength. Instead, I parted my lips and said the one word that I feared I might regret.

The one word that might lead to my heartbreak.

"Sure."

12

VICTORIA

The rest of the week was long and full of meetings. I was exhausted by the time Friday rolled around and I headed out of the office. Even though I was done with my duties as mayor for the week, I knew my week was far from over.

Sawyer had set up a ton of meetings this weekend. When I wasn't out in the town meeting my constituents, I was slotted to attend meals with influential people both in Magnolia and in Newport.

Every moment of my life was booked whether I wanted it to be or not.

Thankfully, Mom and Dad had a pipe burst in their New York condo. They'd left on Wednesday and were still gone. Being home alone with just Danny coming and going was heavenly. My life was beginning to feel as if there was a chance of it returning to normal.

I had my job and my personal space. What more could a girl ask for?

I opened my car door and slid onto the seat just as my phone chimed. I pulled it from my purse and glanced down to see that Clementine had texted the book club group. I swiped my phone to unlock it and read the text.

Clementine: Meet at the dance studio at 5. I have a surprise for you.

I sighed as I slipped my phone back into my purse and started the engine. I really didn't *want* to go over to the dance studio today. I wanted to spend the next few hours curled up on my couch with a book until Sawyer texted to inform me that I needed to meet him for drinks. Right now, I wasn't booked, and I wanted to take advantage of that.

I pulled out of the parking lot, and I should have taken a left to go home, but my curiosity won out and I took a right toward Clem's studio. Everyone else seemed on board with meeting there—my phone continued to chime as I drove. When I pulled into the back parking lot, Shari and Maggie were getting out of their cars at the same time.

Shari looked nervous, and Maggie looked relaxed. I nodded to them, not really interested in having an in-depth conversation with either of them. My quota for interactions with others had reached its limit, and there was no way I wanted to have a forced conversation.

Especially if it meant having to listen to yet another person's problems.

I opened the front door of the studio and held it for Maggie and Shari. They were talking about decorations for the inn and thanked me as they walked through. I kept to the back as I followed behind them.

"Back here," Clementine called from the back room of the studio.

We found her in a small, enclosed room with Fiona. They were standing near a set of poles while music played at a low volume in the background. I immediately wanted to turn and walk out of the room. This wasn't the scene I wanted to walk into.

I'd only agreed to trying out this class back in Maggie's kitchen because I didn't want to be the loser friend who wouldn't try new things. But now that I was standing in the room, facing the prospect of actually trying out one of these poles, my anxiety was through the roof.

The last thing I needed during this reelection campaign was to break a leg. And there was no way I was going to live it down if I injured myself pole dancing. Gravity and I were not friends, and this little dance class was going to prove it.

"Wow. You actually did it," Maggie said as she walked around the poles. She swept her gaze up and down, and her cheeks turned pink.

Well, at least I was not alone in this. She was just as hesitant as I was.

"It's crazy, right? I mean, Jake was concerned as well, but it didn't take him long to figure out a way to anchor them. These babies aren't going anywhere." She reached out and gave them a good shove.

"I can't believe you did it." Shari's voice was low, and I could hear the trepidation in her voice.

The fact that more people than not were nervous about this made me feel confident in turning Clementine down. Sure, we were friends, but we weren't good enough friends for me to risk a broken bone just to please her.

"It's awesome you did this, but there's no way you are getting me up one of those. Who are we kidding? No one wants to see us dancing like this." The words left my lips before I could stop them. I may have come across harsher than I'd intended because as soon as the words left my lips, everyone turned to face me.

I could feel their stares, but I wasn't going to let it bother me. Not now. Not when I had the stress of my parents and this reelection bearing down on me. I met their gazes head-on. Why did they look so shocked? I could tell that most of them did not want to do this either. I was giving them an opportunity to back out. It was up to them to take it.

"Wow," Clementine said. Her excitement had shifted to a cold demeanor. "I'm so excited that I have your support, Victoria." She folded her arms across her chest and moved so that her side faced me. I could tell that I'd hurt her, but I wanted her to be realistic. After all, she was going through all of this effort, and I'd hate to see her burned because of the lack of interest.

"I'm sorry, Clem. I just figured you should know what

you are getting into before you get your hopes up." I could feel myself digging a deeper hole, and even though I wanted to stop myself, it was like a dam had broken inside of me.

I was exhausted and overwhelmed, and my thoughts were not being properly policed. Instead, they were just flowing out of me like word vomit.

"Get my hopes up?" Clementine whipped around until she was staring me down. "How about when I asked you, and you all gave me your support? If you didn't want me to get my hopes up, you should have dashed them back when I floated the idea."

I could see that her eyes were filling with tears, and I wanted to walk back what I'd said. There was no harm in supporting a friend. All I had to do was go to a few classes and then call it quits. I didn't have to say to her what I was saying right now.

"I'll come, Clem. Victoria doesn't speak for me." Maggie stepped up next to Clementine and wrapped her arm around her shoulders.

"And I may not look graceful, but I'm willing to try it out." Shari looked hesitantly over at me and didn't move to take a stand next to Clementine.

Which annoyed me. I didn't need Shari's support. I'd said what I said, sure. But Clementine was getting hurt over nothing.

"Why don't you show us some of the moves you were doing earlier?" Fiona asked. Everyone murmured excitedly, and Clementine sniffled and straightened.

Not wanting to be around these women right now, I mumbled a quick goodbye and hurried from the room, kicking myself as I went.

What I'd said needed to be said. It was about her having realistic expectations for the town of Magnolia. Things ran slower here. I wasn't sure our small town was ready for women hoisting themselves up a pole for fun and recreation.

I was just doing my mayoral duty to her. From the looks of it, none of her other friends were going to do the same.

Once I got out to my car, I pulled open the door and climbed inside. I took a deep breath as I sat there for a moment with my hands on the steering wheel. My entire body felt as if it weighed a million pounds. I just wanted to crawl into a hole and die.

A soft knock on the window drew my attention over. I could see Shari peeking in at me with a smile and a small wave.

I gave her a look that I hoped told her to go away, but she didn't seem interested in listening to me. Instead, she motioned for me to roll down the window. I sighed and started the car. Then I pressed on the window switch and waited.

"You okay?" Shari asked once the window was halfway down.

"I'm great. Why?"

She furrowed her brow, and I silently shushed myself. I didn't need to snap at her. She was just trying to help. But

I felt like I would reach my breaking point any minute now. Even though I hated how I was treating my friends, I was exhausted.

"You just seem tense." Shari met my gaze. "Anything I can help with?"

Maybe a magic genie that could make me mayor and cause my parents to disappear. But I doubted she would enjoy my sarcasm, so I just forced my politician smile and shook my head.

"Nope. I'm good."

Shari didn't look like she believed me, but thankfully, she didn't say anything more. Instead, she just sighed and backed up from my car. I gave her a salute, and just as I started to pull out of the parking spot, she called out, "You can always reach out to me if you need anything."

Her words tugged at my heart. There was a certain camaraderie that came from the women in Magnolia. Despite not always speaking or spending time with each other, we were always there for one another. That was what being a small town was all about.

But I hated the fact that they were acting this way toward me. I was the strong one. I was the mayor. I had the education and the experience. I wasn't supposed to be one who didn't have her life figured out. I was supposed to be the one helping other people figure out their future.

I hated that even though I wasn't the broken one, I felt like I was.

With every moment that ticked by, I was breaking more and more.

When I got home, I snuck into the kitchen and up to my room. I wasn't ready to face anyone right now. Not when I felt this way. Not when I was this unhappy.

Once I was behind my closed door, I let out the breath I'd been holding. I wished I could say that my stress went with my exhaled breath, but it didn't. It stayed sandwiched between my shoulder blades, desperate to never let go.

I scrubbed my face as I padded over to my bathroom and started the shower. Steam and hot water seemed like the antidote to my pain—the pain that came from trying to meet everyone's expectations but realizing that, even after all you tried to do, you could never be enough.

I was beginning to think *I* was never going to be enough.

No matter how much I wished that weren't true, the reality of my situation was weighing down on me and making it impossible for me to feel happy. I was getting to the point that I wasn't even sure what happiness felt like anymore.

I cried silently while I stood in the shower, letting the water beat down on my face and shoulders. The water mixed with my tears, and while I stood here, I could pretend that I wasn't crying, that I didn't feel broken.

But I knew the truth.

And that truth scared me.

If I faced it, did that mean I was accepting defeat? If I admitted to myself that I just might not be enough for anyone, where did that leave me?

Reality washed over me as I flipped off the shower. After I wrapped my wet, dripping hair up into a towel and wrapped another around my body, I stepped out of the shower and onto my plush bath mat.

Steam clouded the mirror, and the only thing I could see was a fuzzy version of myself. As I stared at my outline, I knew the truth of what I didn't want to admit.

It was one small word that had me feeling terrified.

Alone.

That's where admitting my faults got me. Alone with nothing to distract me from my pain.

And that was a fate that was worse than death. At least for me.

If I wanted to survive, I needed to play the game. I needed to put on a brave face and work even harder to achieve my dreams.

Because the true and real Victoria was not someone anyone wanted to meet. She was the girl they ran from in elementary school and the one they backstabbed in high school and college.

She was the girl that boys didn't want to stick around for and the one her parents were never going accept.

She was the girl I'd spent my life hiding, and there was no way I was going to let her out now.

She was buried deep down, and I was going to try with all my might to keep her buried. For good.

She was never going to emerge.

Not if I could help it.

13

SHARI

I wanted to linger at Clementine's studio and brainstorm things we could do to help Victoria, but I needed to get home so I could get ready for my date with Danny.

Butterflies erupted inside of me as I repeated that one word in my mind over and over again.

Date. Date.

I had a *date* with Danny.

Me. Single mom, divorcée Shari had a date with Magnolia's most eligible bachelor.

My cheeks flushed as Danny's face floated into my mind, and despite my efforts, he refused to leave. All I could see were his dark eyes and half smile as I stared at Clementine. She was talking—but I wasn't registering what she was saying.

"You okay?" Maggie whispered as she leaned closer to me and nudged me with her shoulder.

I startled and glanced in her direction. Her smile was soft as she ran her gaze over me. "Yeah, I'm fine," I said softly, but a giggle erupted, and I slammed my lips together.

"Did you just giggle?" Maggie asked, this time louder as she moved to face me.

"No." If I denied it, that meant it didn't happen, right?

"You totally did. I heard it."

"Heard what?" Clementine broke away from her conversation with Fiona and moved to stand next to us.

"Nothing." There was no way I needed Clementine knowing what was happening to me. She would tell Jake, and then either Jake would never let me live it down, or he'd give Danny some strange big-brother lecture.

"It is not nothing. Shari giggled." Maggie was no help. When I narrowed my eyes in her direction, she just shrugged. "I call it like I see it."

I sighed as I glanced between Clementine, Fiona, and Maggie.

As much as I wanted Victoria to be here—I suspected that her reaction to Clementine meant something deeper was going on—I was kind of glad she'd stormed off. I was already struggling with telling these women that I was going on a date with Danny—having his older sister here would have only make it that much harder.

"Does it have to do with tonight?" Clementine asked.

I wanted to groan. I'd asked her to babysit. That was my first mistake. But Carol was out of town, and there was no way I wanted to call Danny up and ask him to reschedule because I couldn't find a babysitter.

I wasn't ready for him to be that privy to my life.

At least, not yet.

"No," I lied when I realized that Clementine's question had piqued everyone's interest. They were all leaning closer to me as if waiting to hear the answer.

"I think it does." Maggie glanced between Clem and Fiona. "What do we think? A date?"

"Most definitely a date. Look at how red her ears are getting," Fiona said as she waved toward my head.

I instantly covered them with my hands. "They are not."

"And her cheeks. Let's not forget about her cheeks."

Now all three women were leaning in closer to me as they inspected my body.

Ready to get the heck out of here, I stepped back and moved to grab my purse, which I'd set on the floor. "If you're done, I need to get back home—"

"For your date." Maggie interjected.

I shot her an annoyed look. "No. Unless you call spending time with my kids a date." I shouldered my purse and headed toward the front door. It felt like miles away with how silent the room was.

"Jake and I will be over at seven to watch your kids for your non-date," Clementine called after me.

I already had the door open and was stepping outside when I caught what she said. Not wanting another embarrassing reaction to spread so plainly across my face, I waved my hand in her direction and slipped the rest of the way outside.

Now alone, I let out a deep breath and pulled my suit coat tighter around my body. My nerves, mixed with the cool evening air, left me shivering. Thankfully, Jake didn't ask any questions when I collected my children. They were hanging out with him at the hardware store, eating caramels and throwing darts.

It made me happy that my brother seemed to be adjusting well to his new life. He was growing his beard out and wearing flannel shirts. He looked like the epitome of a small-town hardware store owner.

I thought about teasing him but then decided against it. After all, the longer I stayed, the less time I had to get ready and the more likely it was for him to ask me questions about tonight.

For all he knew, I was spending the evening alone, and honestly, that was all I needed him to think. Especially since I was sure, the minute Clementine got around him, she was going to spill whatever she thought I was doing.

"Come on, guys," I called from the front door.

Bella and Tag groaned in unison. Frustration built up inside of me as I took a few more steps into the store. There was no way I wanted to drag them away, but if that was what I needed to do, I'd do it.

Jake appeared in the aisle next to me. He grinned as he took a few steps and scooped me up into a hug. "I can keep them here for the night if you want."

There was a cheer from the cash register.

I sighed as I pulled back and gave him a look. I didn't want him to see how relieved his offer made me feel. Without my kids around, asking me questions about where I was going, I just might be able to calm myself down long enough to make it through this night.

"Really?" I asked, making sure to steel my expression.

Jake chuckled. "Yeah, sure. We don't have many evenings left where it is going to be this warm. I was thinking about setting up the projector and playing a movie with a bonfire and popcorn."

Bella and Tag whooped in agreement.

Jake laughed as he glanced over his shoulder at them. "See? I knew it would be a hit."

I couldn't fight the smile playing on my lips any longer. I loved having my brother around. He made my life easier and helped me to feel more relaxed. An overwhelming feeling of gratitude took over, and I didn't fight it as I reached out and wrapped my arms around his waist. "Thanks," I whispered.

Jake hesitated before he chuckled and gave me a squeeze. "Wow. You feeling all right?" he asked as he pulled back and peeked down at me. I loved his comforting smile and how happy he seemed. Ever since he and Clementine got back together, he was more relaxed. Like this was the place he belonged. I just wished I could feel the same.

I sighed and nodded as I pulled away. "Yeah, I'm feeling good. Just tired."

Jake nodded as he motioned toward my face. "I wasn't going to say anything, but those bags under your eyes..."

I walloped him in the arm as he let his voice trail off. Typical Jake.

"Owie," he said as he moved to protect his arm. "No need to get violent."

"I'm leaving," I called over my shoulder as I walked over to my kids and gave each of them a kiss on the top of their heads—despite their protests. Then I shouldered my purse and headed toward the door.

"I'll bring them home tomorrow morning," Jake called after me.

I nodded and pushed through the door. Once I was outside, I paused and watched as Jake made his way toward Bella and Tag. They were laughing at something he said as he rested his elbows on the table, his goofy smile beaming in their direction.

My chest squeezed, and for a moment, I felt guilty for leaving my kids. After all, they were just beginning to adjust to our new life—well, Bella more than Tag. Did it make me a terrible mother to just abandon them with my brother? Should I stick around?

It took me a moment of wallowing in my guilt before I pulled myself from my thoughts and focused on my car. I would drive home, get ready, and allow myself a night out with Danny. When it went bad—and I was fairly certain it was going to go bad—then I could move forward. I wouldn't have regrets. This was my one chance at returning to the dating world, and if it didn't work out, then at least I would know.

By the time I got home, my nerves were on edge. I showered and stood in front of my closet in a towel as I stared at my clothes. Nothing looked right. Everything screamed *mom* instead of *available*.

Ugh. This was a huge mistake.

I contemplated texting Danny and telling him that I couldn't go out tonight. All sorts of excuses ran through my mind as I picked up and set down my phone a few times. Then I shook my head and mustered my courage as I settled on a black dress with a blush-pink jacket.

I applied my makeup, trying to remember all the evening eyes Clementine had told me about. By the time I was done, I looked like a raccoon, so I quickly washed it off and settled on just foundation and mascara—my go-to look.

After I dried my hair, I curled it slightly. I was attempting to go with beach waves, but I wasn't sure if I did it right. After fiddling with it for the tenth time, I blew out my breath and unplugged my curling iron, shut off the bathroom light, and made my way into my bedroom.

I was done getting ready, and if I tried to fix anything, I was just going to make it worse.

I slipped on my dark-blue mid-ankle boots. As I used my dresser to steady myself, my fingers brushed the brown envelope that I'd set there a week ago. Once my feet were in my shoes, I straightened and allowed my gaze to fall on the envelope.

My divorce papers.

I was going to need to sign them. Especially since I was headed out this evening with another man.

Guilt and frustration with myself weighed down on my chest as I swallowed back the tears that threatened to emerge. I'd worked so hard to get ready, there was no way I wanted to undo any of my effort.

Not wanting my lack of action to stare me in the face anymore, I opened the top drawer of my dresser and slipped the envelope under my folded pajamas. Then I shut the drawer and leaned against my dresser, taking the time to breathe in a few deep breaths.

Even though I was essentially hiding from my responsibilities, there was a sort of calm that came over me when I realized that I'd actually taken action. I'd done something with the past that clung to me everywhere I went. The removal of those divorce papers from my line of sight felt freeing in a way that I couldn't describe.

Feeling lighter and happier, I headed down the stairs just as my doorbell rang. Butterflies took flight as I made my way over to the door and peeked out the side window. Danny was standing there in a leather jacket, dark jeans, and black shoes. His hair was styled but still looked touchable.

My heart pounded as I took him in. I wanted to open the door, but another part of me wanted to keep it shut. I didn't want to disappoint him. After looking at what he had to offer, the feeling that I was sorely lacking in the appearance department started to rise up inside of me.

I must have drifted off in my thoughts, because a moment later, Danny appeared in my line of sight. He was leaning down, and his smile made me feel so warm and welcome—even if I was completely embarrassed that he'd caught me staring at him.

"You gonna let me in?" he asked, his voice muffled by the glass.

My cheeks flushed as I straightened and nodded. Then I turned the handle and opened the door on Danny's full frame. His shoulders were so broad, and he was so tall, that he took up most of the doorway. I felt tiny in his presence, especially when he stepped forward and into the entryway. He smelled amazing, and I couldn't help but take in a deep breath.

Thankfully, Danny didn't hesitate—he didn't seem as discombobulated as I was. He shut the door behind him and took a step closer to me as he peered down with his sexy half smile teasing his lips. His perfect lips that I couldn't help but allow my gaze to drop down to.

"You look amazing," he said. There was this look in his gaze. A look that said he appreciated what he was seeing. It made me feel warm and worried at the same time. If he was looking at me—truly looking—what would he find? Would he discover how broken I really was?

Would he be disappointed?

"You're the one who looks amazing." The words tumbled from my lips before I could police them. I pinched my lips together as I peeked up at him to see that his smile hadn't faltered.

He wiggled his eyebrows when his gaze met mine. "You think I look amazing?" he asked, inching closer to me again.

I'd retreated as far back as I could go. My back was pressed against the wall, but that didn't seem to stop Danny. Instead, he towered over me. I could feel his warmth even though he was still inches away. I was certain he could hear my heart galloping in my chest. I wanted to reach out. I wanted to touch him. I wanted to feel alive again. And I had this sinking suspicion that he was the man to help me do that.

But I was scared. Scared of the scars that I was trying to hide. Scared that I wasn't who he wanted. That somehow he'd deluded himself into thinking he wanted me, but when the truth came out, he'd discover that he'd made a mistake. And I'd be left behind with nothing once more.

"We should get going," I said as I turned and slipped away from him. I straightened my jacket and offered him a warm smile. One that said I wasn't expecting anything. All we were doing was going out as friends and nothing more.

Danny looked a tad disappointed as he turned and clapped his hands together. But that didn't last long before he moved to open the front door. He held it for me and motioned toward his car, which he'd parked in my drive-way. "M'lady," he said with a deep drawl and a wink as he leaned forward in a bow.

I laughed for the first time in a long time. It was free

and unabated. Despite my fears, I could feel my stress lighten as I watched his smile spread. We walked side by side to his car, where he opened the passenger door and waited for me to get in.

Once we were on the road, I felt myself continue to lighten as I watched the trees pass by. Danny seemed to want to keep where we were going a secret, and I kind of liked that. I liked not having to stress about where we were going or what we were going to do. I liked the fact that I didn't have to plan our evening.

Craig had always made me find the babysitter and make the reservations. So the fact that Danny had taken responsibility for everything made me feel lighter. It made me feel...special. And that was a feeling I hadn't gotten in a long time.

We crossed the bridge into Newport, and Danny pulled up to the valet service of some fancy restaurant I'd never been to before. He climbed out of the driver's side and tossed the keys to the valet who was approaching. They seemed to know each other as they laughed and exchanged greetings.

It amazed me that Danny seemed so relaxed wherever he went. It had to be who his family was. After all, he was a Holt. Hospitality and connections ran in their blood. It was his birthright to go to places like this and to know people like the valet.

I, on the other hand, spent most of my life driving up and down parking lots, waiting for a car to leave so I could get a closer spot. Rolling up to a restaurant and having someone park the car for me felt so foreign that I was beginning to feel uncomfortable. Was this where I belonged? Was I deluding myself into thinking that I was going to be able to fit into Danny's life?

And then I pushed those fears away. I wasn't trying to fit into Danny's life. This was just a one-night thing. One date, and then we would part ways. After all, I was sure that at some point tonight, Danny was going to discover the kind of disaster that my life was. He was going to see the drama that my past and future held, and he was going to split. And honestly, I wouldn't blame him.

I was disappointed in myself as well.

The passenger door opened, and Danny's grinning face appeared. "We're here," he said, extending his hand to help me out.

I paused and then gathered my courage as I slipped my hand into his. Danny continued holding my hand as we stood side by side, facing the restaurant. He seemed so calm while I was this jumbled mess.

Why couldn't I relax?

As if he felt my need for reassurance, Danny took my hand and moved it to the crook of his arm. He closed the gap between his arm and chest, effectively pinning my arm next to him. As if he felt my desire to run away and was trying to convince me otherwise.

He glanced down at me, and I could feel his smile as he studied me. "Ready?" he asked.

I sucked in my breath and forced myself to be stronger than I felt. After all, I didn't want to be this weak forever.

Craig had broken me, but it was up to me to try to fix the pain I felt every day. I was determined to reimagine myself, and that started with me regaining the confidence I'd lost. The confidence that Craig had taken from me.

"Yes," I whispered as I turned to face him.

Danny gave me a wink and led me into the restaurant.

There was no turning back now. I was going to eat dinner with Danny. The beginning of the new Shari started right now.

Whether I was ready or not.

14

SHARI

D inner was delicious. Despite looking fancier than I was used to, the restaurant had a simplistic menu of mouthwatering food. I chose a surf and turf meal, and the steak and lobster melted in my mouth. I found myself eating more than I was talking, which Danny didn't seem to mind.

He spent most of dinner devouring his food as well.

I was so stuffed by the time I was done, I felt as if I were going to explode. Danny was the same as he leaned back and rubbed his stomach. His expression depicted exactly how I felt. Full and happy.

"That was amazing," I said as I set my fork down on my plate. Our waitress came by to whisk it away, and another waiter dropped off a new glass of wine. I contemplated drinking it before I stopped myself. I was already feeling tipsy, and with how satisfied my full stomach made me feel, I feared what I might do when I felt this good.

I needed my wits about me if I was going to survive the rest of this date.

Danny chuckled. "I'm glad you enjoyed it."

I decided to throw caution to the wind and picked up the wine glass. I tipped my head back and let the liquid slip into my mouth and down my throat. "Craig would have never taken me to a place like this," I said as I set the glass down. Then, realizing that I'd brought up my ex-husband, I pinched my lips together and glanced in Danny's direction.

Did he hear me?

From his furrowed brow, I could tell that he had. Crap.

"Craig?" he asked as he met my gaze.

I needed to do some damage control. "My ex-husband."

"Ah."

Feeling the need to be honest with him, I decided to part my lips and let the truth flow. If Danny was even a little bit interested in me, then he needed to hear it all. Unfiltered.

"I'm divorced..." I pinched my lips at that lie. "Well, I will be. Once I sign the papers." My cheeks were warm as I felt Danny's gaze. What was he thinking? Was he disappointed? "And I have two kids. Bella and Tag." I let those words linger in the air as I studied him. I half expected him to get up and walk away from me.

Which, if I were honest with myself, I wouldn't have

blamed him for doing. After all, he'd probably figured I was someone else. And now that he knew the truth, I doubted he wanted to stick around for more.

And then he did something that I hadn't been expecting. He smiled. Not in a creepy Joker kind of way. Instead, it was soft and full of relief.

He made no attempt to explain his reaction as he pushed away from the table and stood. Then he rounded the table and made his way over to me with his hand extended. "Come with me," he said softly.

I stared at him and then down at his hand. What was going on? This was not the reaction that I'd expected. Not at all.

But not wanting to appear weak, I nodded, slipped my hand into his, and stood up from the table. On our way out, we passed by the hostess, who informed Danny she would bill the card on file. He nodded but didn't stop as he led me out of the restaurant and over to the valet stand. The valet didn't wait for instructions. Instead, he just nodded to us and disappeared through the door of the parking lot next to the restaurant.

Danny and I stood there in silence. He was holding my hand with more possession this time. As if he were no longer afraid that I was going to slip away. Instead, it was as if he wanted me to know his intentions, but I wasn't sure if I was ready to dissect what those intentions might be.

We were in his car and driving down the road before I knew it, and even though he seemed calm, I still felt confused as to what was going on. I thought my revelation would have had him running for the hills. But it seemed to have had the exact opposite effect. Or he was such a gentleman that he wanted to make sure that he took me home before he ditched me, never to be seen again.

Regardless, I couldn't relax until he told me what was going on.

About ten minutes later, Danny pulled into a parking lot off the freeway and turned off the engine. He glanced over at me and smiled. "Come on," he said softly.

I glanced around. The ocean was about a hundred feet from where we were parked. The moon was glistening off the surface. I opened my door, allowing the smell of salt and the feeling of crisp autumn air to surround me. "Is this where you kill me?" I asked as I stepped out and shut the door behind me.

Danny was digging around in the trunk, and he peeked around the car to smile at me. "Yes," he said in a flirting way.

"I knew it." I rounded the corner to see that Danny had what looked like tissue paper in his hands.

He slammed the trunk, shifted the items to one arm, and grabbed hold of my hand with his now free one. Shivers exploded across my skin, and I reveled in the feeling of his gesture. It was as if he were no longer shy about touching me. I liked that he seemed confident enough to take charge.

In fact, I kind of loved it. It made me feel special. It made me feel like a woman. And I missed feeling like that.

When we got to the beach, we took off our shoes even though the sand was cool. I had to quicken my pace to keep up with him as he led me to the water's edge and stopped.

"What are we doing?" I asked as he set the items he'd been holding down next to him.

He glanced up at me with a mischievous smile. "You'll see."

I watched as he opened the tissue paper to reveal that they were in fact lanterns. The kind that you lit and they floated up into the air. He handed me one and then opened a second lantern and set it down on the ground next to him.

"What are we doing?" I asked as he opened a few more and lined them up.

He chuckled. "Have you heard of wish lanterns?"

"Wish lanterns?"

He nodded as he motioned to the one I was holding. "It's said that if you make a wish and light the lantern, your wish will come true."

I turned the lantern around in my hands. "Really?"

"It's science."

I snorted.

He shot me a look. "I'm serious. There is no documented wish that didn't come true when wished with a lantern." He wiggled his eyebrows and gave me a wink.

"Sounds accurate," I teased. Then I waved to the five lanterns on the ground. "And you can do this over and over?"

He glanced at the lanterns and then back at me. "Maybe. Maybe not. But I figured why risk it? Give yourself numerous chances to have a wish granted."

I liked his thinking.

Before I could respond, he neared me with a lighter in hand. Instead of pulling back when he got close, he leaned into it, hovering next to me so he could light the small circle in the middle of the lantern. His arm brushed mine. I could smell his cologne. I could feel his body warmth cascade over me.

It intoxicated me and awoke a desire that scared me. That made me want to pull away. This wasn't supposed to happen. I was supposed to be alone forever. Craig had proven to me that I wasn't worth sticking around for. That there was an inherent flaw within me that he'd needed to compensate for with another woman.

Danny wasn't supposed to want to be close to me. Didn't he realize that?

He lingered by me for a moment longer. Despite my desire to protect myself, I allowed my gaze to trail up to his, and I held it there for a moment. His expression was so warm, and there was a heat in the way he looked at me that took my breath away.

Did I dare allow myself to hope that it meant what I wanted it to mean?

"Are you ready?" he asked. His voice has shifted. It was low and throaty. As if he were reacting to our proximity like I was.

"Ready?" I asked. I was whispering now. If I spoke

louder, would he spook? Would I wake up from this dream?

"To make a wish." He stepped back, taking his warmth with him. I shivered involuntarily as the desire for him to come back washed over me.

But as he moved farther away, my mind began to clear, and I was brought back to the present and what we were here to do.

Release the lanterns. One of which was lit and in my hands.

I glanced down and stared at the flame as it flickered in front of me. Danny wanted me to make a wish. But what did I wish for? My life was already in shambles. Did I allow myself to hope that a spoken desire mixed with a lantern could actually fix the problems that bogged me down?

Suddenly, two arms surrounded me from behind, and Danny's large and warm hands enveloped my own. His chest pressed against my back as he moved closer to me.

"It's just a wish," he said softly.

His warm breath tickled my skin as his lips lingered next to my ear.

"Just a wish?" I asked so quietly that I doubted he could hear me. But I felt his head nod next to mine.

"Just a wish," he repeated. "Close your eyes and say what your heart wants."

I didn't hesitate as I let my eyes flutter closed. What my heart wanted. What did it want? Tears pricked my eyes as I thought about the last year. What it had done to me.

What it had done to my family. I'd been so lost and alone for so long, that I'd forgotten how to think for myself. How to want something for me.

What did that feel like? Was I ready to allow it?

And then, deep down, a flicker emerged. It was a glimmer of what I really wanted. It wasn't something that I could find in a store or that someone could give me. It was something that I needed to do for myself.

I wanted to be happy. Truly and wholly happy.

I was tired of feeling down on myself. For hating what Craig had done to me. For feeling broken and destroyed. I wanted to let that all go and begin again.

So I squeezed my eyes tightly shut and took in a deep breath. "I want to be happy," I whispered as I opened my eyes and released the lantern into the air. I watched as it floated up into the sky, taking my wish with it.

Danny's hands moved to my waist as he pulled me in closer. My breath caught in my throat as he held me. So intimate, and yet, I could feel his support. His desire to be close to me washed across my entire body.

"You want to be happy?" he asked. His voice was so low and sexy that it was doing things to me that I was too embarrassed to admit.

Danny was a man. Unlike the man I'd married. Danny was something else entirely. He knew how to hold a woman. He knew how to be close to her. He made me feel like I was a woman. And I needed to feel like that. More than I'd realized before.

"Yes," I said softly.

He tightened his embrace. "What does that look like?"

Fire erupted inside of me. A desire to act. I was tired of feeling weak. I was tired of berating myself. Of telling myself that I wasn't good enough for Danny. He seemed to want me like I wanted him. Why was I so shy about allowing myself to want again?

Had Craig ruined me this much?

At some point, I was going to need to let what happened go. I was going to need to face the future—whatever that meant.

Before I could talk myself out of acting, I slipped around until I was facing Danny. He looked surprised, but he didn't loosen his grasp on me. Instead, his hands found the small of my back, and he held me there. Despite my desire to move his hands so he couldn't feel the rolls that resided there, I pushed those thoughts away and lingered against his chest.

My hands found his chest, and I sprawled my fingers out so I could feel his muscles, his breathing, and his heart beating in time with mine. He was as nervous as I was—which made me happy. I wasn't alone in my insecurities.

"Do you want to see what happiness looks like to me?" I asked as I allowed my gaze to trail from his eyes down to his lips, where the desire to kiss them burned inside of me.

"Yes," he said, his voice turning husky.

So I acted. I threw aside all of my worries and doubts as I rose up onto my tiptoes and pressed my lips to his. At first, I wasn't sure what to do. Had I shocked him? He wasn't moving, and neither was I. It was as if we were each trying to figure out the other.

And then slowly, softly, Danny brought his hand up to my cheek and cradled it. He began to move his lips against mine. That was all the confirmation I needed. I dragged my hands up his chest to the nape of his neck and entwined my fingers in his hair.

He groaned and parted his lips. His tongue slid into my mouth, which only caused the hunger inside of me to intensify. I wanted this. No, I needed this. Excitement mixed with fear was an intoxicating concoction. Part of me knew I needed to back away while the other part wanted more.

So much more.

His hands found my waist, and he pressed them into my back, pulling me closer to him. I could feel his body's warmth as it washed over mine. I wanted to touch and feel every part of him.

Throwing caution to the wind, I fisted his shirt in my hands as I pulled him down to the sandy ground beneath us. He chuckled as he obediently followed. I lay on the ground as Danny towered over me. His hip was against my side, but his arms were around me as they caged me in.

His lips never left mine as we fell into a dance. His tongue played against mine, causing my heart to pound out of control. This was what kissing felt like. This was what it felt like to be wanted by a man. I'd never felt this kind of passion from Craig. This fire of desire that raged inside of me.

I wanted more of Danny. I wanted all of Danny.

When he broke the kiss, I groaned, pulling myself up to meet him again. He chuckled as he obliged me for a moment longer before breaking off. "I need a minute," he said. He didn't move to get off of me. Instead, he lingered above me, smiling as his gaze raked over my face.

I suddenly felt shy. Never in my life had I allowed myself to be so open and so raw with someone else. I'd shown him my heart, and now I was terrified what he was going to do with it.

"Why the furrow?" he asked as he dusted off his hands and used the tips of his fingers to trace the center of my brows.

"Furrow?" I asked, reaching up to feel my forehead.

He nodded. "You look worried."

I swallowed, hating that my insecurities were so plainly written across my face. I closed my eyes for a moment as I took in a deep breath. I needed to be confident. Danny was going to be turned off by me if I wasn't the confident woman that he deserved.

"I'm not worried," I said quietly.

His lips pressed against mine, startling me into opening my eyes once more. But he didn't move to end the kiss, so I fell into the confidence that I got from being next to him. A confidence that came from having him care for me.

I lost myself in our kiss. I lost myself in the way that I felt for him. I lost myself in the strength that I gained from having him next to me. The strength I got from the idea that, perhaps, I was no longer confined by the life I thought I had to live, and instead, I could live the one that I wanted to live.

The one that was no longer controlled by Craig. It was controlled by me. I got to decide if I was happy or not. I got to decide if I was going to take chances. I got to decide if I was going to allow myself to enjoy my time with Danny.

To feel what I felt when he kissed me. When he wrapped his arms around me.

Tomorrow, I would wake up and face my life. Tomorrow, I was going to be Shari, mom and vice principal.

But for tonight, with Danny's arms wrapped around me like I was the only woman in the world that mattered, I was going to just be Shari.

And I was ready to just be Shari.

15

VICTORIA

S awyer was on a rampage. I could tell he was annoyed with something or someone when I made my way into work Monday morning. He was pacing in my office, and I could see him moving back and forth when I walked up to Brooke's desk. I glanced at her to see that her eyes were wide.

She knew something that I didn't.

If I were honest with myself, I didn't really want to know what was going on. I was still reeling over my outburst at the book club ladies, and even though Maggie tried to reach out with some sort of peace offering, I didn't call her back.

I was wallowing, and that was all I wanted to do. I didn't need a pep talk from the ladies. I wanted peace and quiet. I spent my weekend curled up in bed with choco-lates and the Hallmark channel. Mom and Dad were back from the city and didn't seem interested in me, and Danny had been MIA most of the weekend. Whatever he was doing had him distracted.

I'd be angry at him for abandoning me if he didn't look so happy during those few fleeting moments that I actually saw him. I'd never seen him look so grounded and at peace. Whatever hobby he'd discovered, I was happy that at least he was feeling fulfilled—even if I wasn't.

But I knew ignoring Sawyer until he went away was a pipe dream. He wasn't going to leave until he told me whatever bad news he was chewing on, so I might as well focus and get it over with.

"What's going on in there?" I asked Brooke as I took the stack of messages that she'd collected for me and riffled through them. They were mostly your basic citizen complaints. Dogs barking. Property line disputes. Things I could take care of once I figured out what had Sawyer looking like he was about to kill someone.

Brooke pinched her lips together. "It's not good."

I glanced over at Sawyer. "You going to tell me, or do I have to walk in there unarmed."

Brooke sighed and leaned forward as if she were telling me a secret. "Peter just announced that he's running for mayor as well."

My entire body went numb as I stared at Brooke. My ears were ringing as if my body were trying to reject the words she just said to me. "Peter?" I finally managed to squeak out. "As in Peter Tippens?"

I lost my valedictorian spot in high school to a new move-in that came to us all the way from New York. My family may be well-known in town, but the Tippens were like royalty. It had been a relief when Peter moved away, going to some Ivy League college and landing a high-ranking job in the government.

Dad lamented about his family climbing the political ranks, but I never let it bother me. Not when it didn't affect me. After all, Peter wasn't here, so what did it matter?

But now, my armpits were sweating, and heat was pricking the back of my neck. This couldn't be happening. Not when my life felt like it was falling apart.

I swallowed as I made my way over to the coffee pot and poured myself a mug. After loading it up with sugar and more creamer than I cared to admit, I leaned against the counter and took some deep breaths, inhaling the scent and hoping it would ground me.

This was no big deal. I could handle this. Peter may be royalty, but I'd given my life to this town. That had to count for something.

Sawyer must have seen me, because my office door was flung open, and a moment later, he was standing next to me. His nervous energy caused my stomach to flip as I focused on sipping my mug of creamer with a bit of coffee in it.

"Peter Tippens just announced his run," Sawyer said. His cheeks were pink, and he was huffing and puffing as he stood there. He looked panicked, and I didn't like that. He was supposed to tell me that it was no big deal. That I was going to be able to overcome this and be victorious.

But he was staring at me like the world had gone down the toilet, and I was beginning to doubt my own ability. I hated that. I already got so much doubt from Mom and Dad that the last thing I needed was to have yet another person in my life seeing me as less than.

I could conquer whatever Peter Tippens tossed my direction. I could. I just needed to get out of my head and trudge forward.

"So let's strategize. What's the plan from here?" I asked, forcing myself to sound more confident than I actually felt. I was faltering, and if I gave in to that self-doubt, I was pretty sure that I wasn't going to be able to survive.

Sawyer took in a few deep breaths as he rubbed his temples and closed his eyes. He looked as if he were coming back from the ledge, which I was grateful for. We were going to be able to come up with a solution. *I* was going to be fine.

"Right. Right," he repeated as he straightened and nodded in my direction. "We're going to be fine. We can handle this."

I patted his shoulder. "We can." I gave him a soft smile. "We've dealt with worse."

"We have."

Sawyer coming around was helping to take some of the stress off my shoulders. If I could convince him, then he could support me, and we'd make it through this setback together.

Pushing my pity party to the side, I motioned for Sawyer to follow me into my office. I wasn't one to go down without a fight, and Peter was going to rue the day that he decided to run against me. I had determination and grit, and there was no way I was going to lose to him again.

I was going to be the victorious one this time.

"Let's strategize," I said as I set my coffee down and sat on my desk chair. I pulled myself up so I could rest my elbows on my desk, steepling my fingers.

Sawyer collapsed into the chair across from me. "Well, we should schedule some more interviews. I was thinking we could take out an ad in the paper, and you could do an interview on Magnolia Today."

I nodded. Local channels meant local exposure. Problem was funds were running low. The last thing I wanted was to ask my parents for money, and not a lot of people were lining up to donate to my campaign. Which was fine before Peter showed up. After all, who was I campaigning against? If people didn't have a strong second choice, then I was the winner by default.

Now, things were changing.

My conversation with Collin Kerston entered my mind. His invitation to eat together floated around in my mind. If I met with him, perhaps he'd be willing to contribute. I had to at least try.

"What's that face for?" Sawyer asked as he leaned forward. "Do you have an idea?"

I pulled my phone from my purse and swiped it on. "I think I have a donor," I said as I located Collin's number and pressed on it. After a short conversation with his assistant, I left a message with her, asking if Collin could meet me for lunch. She said she would give him the message, and I hung up.

Sawyer looked less stressed when I set my phone on my desk and glanced up at him. He had brought up his foot onto his other knee and was fiddling with his shoe. I could tell that he was still nervous, but he was working through his anxiety. Which I was grateful for. It helped me relax.

"Lunch with Kerston Pharmacy?" Sawyer asked.

I nodded.

"I like that plan."

————

I was surprised how quickly Collin got back to me. He texted and agreed to meet me wherever I wanted to go. Not wanting the whole town to see me meet with Collin, I told him that I wanted to try out the new chef at the inn, and we agreed to meet at noon.

When I pulled into the parking lot at 11:45, I let my engine idle as I sat there. I took in a few deep breaths as I tried to calm the butterflies that were attacking my stomach. I could do this. I was strong and confident. The fact that I'd somehow lost control of that frustrated me.

I couldn't be weak. I couldn't.

Who would I be if I wasn't hard-nosed Victoria?

I'd spent too long being the girl that never admitted defeat. I was the girl who always dominated because she wanted it more. And really, I wanted to be reelected, but the pressure to perform like this was starting to get to me.

And I was beginning to doubt I could survive this forever.

Once the election was over, the stress would lessen. I needed to remind myself of that. I was only overwhelmed because I was trying to fight a battle. This feeling wasn't going to last forever.

I slipped my fingers into the door release and pushed out into the cool, salty air. I straightened, pressing my hands into my back and forcing the tension that resided there from my muscles. I wasn't going to win Collin over if I rolled up to our meeting all stressed and tense.

If I was going to gain his endorsement and donation, I needed to look smooth and collected.

I slammed the door and shouldered my purse. I crossed the parking lot and made my way up the front steps and through the large, wooden doors. The inn was quiet as I lingered in the foyer.

There were a few people sitting in the living room off to the side, but that was it. I was grateful for the scarcity. It meant I was going to be able to have a private meeting.

"Victoria?" Maggie's voice caused me to turn as she walked up to me. She was wearing an apron that was dusted with flour.

"Hello, Maggie," I said in the best mayoral voice I could muster.

That just caused Maggie to look confused as she

glanced around. "What are you doing here? Do you need a room?"

I shook my head. "No. Nothing like that. I'm actually here for a business lunch. You said I had to come try the food." I extended my hands. "So I'm here."

Maggie looked slightly relieved as she nodded and dusted her hands on her apron. "Well, we're glad to have you." She waved her hand toward the dining room.

I followed behind her as she led me over to a table in the corner of the room. It was right next to the large picture windows, where a picturesque view of the ocean greeted me.

If I weren't here to meet Collin, I might have requested to have my food outside, where I could take off my shoes and dig my feet into the sand. Even though it was fall, there was still some warmth in the air.

It sounded relaxing and exactly like what I needed, until reality surrounded me once more, and I brought my attention back to the room I was standing in. There was an older couple enjoying some sort of pastry while drinking coffee and whispering to each other. A man who looked as if he were here on a business trip was sitting on the couch in the living room with his laptop resting in his lap.

Everyone looked more at ease than me. They didn't look as if they were carrying the weight of the world on their shoulders.

Once I was settled at the table, Maggie said she would be right back with water and menus. I nodded and allowed myself to relax against the chair as my gaze wandered back toward the window. I could see the waves of the ocean as it moved against the shore.

It was mesmerizing to watch the movement. Even though I was separated by glass from the sound, I could hear the crashing of the waves just by looking at them. There was something so soothing and healing about watching the ocean that the stress that had coated my muscles began to lessen.

I felt as if I could breathe again.

Maggie returned sans apron. She had menus tucked against her hip and carried two water glasses on a tray. I thanked her as I took a menu from her, and she set the waters down.

She lingered, and I attempted to pretend that I couldn't see her, even though she was making herself quite obvious as she stood there. Her stare was piercing, and I began to get the feeling that she was not going to leave until I addressed her.

"What's up, Mags?" I asked as I set down my menu and turned to focus on her.

That just caused her eyebrows to rise as her eyes widened. "Do you really not know?"

I blew out my breath. I knew what she wanted to talk about. But I didn't want to discuss what had happened with Clementine. At least, not right now. Not when my life felt like it was falling apart no matter how hard I tried to keep it together. My control was slipping, and I didn't like that feeling. It caused me to lash out, and the last thing I wanted to do was alienate my friends.

Or, whom I thought were my friends. It was still up for debate. I mean, they were nice to me. They allowed me to attend their book club. But would they call me their friend? I wasn't sure. And that uncertainty didn't sit well with me.

Maggie didn't wait for me to respond. She pulled out the chair in front of her and sat down. Her gaze never left my face as she leaned in. "Clementine is really worried that you are upset with her. She's about to have Jake pull down the poles." Maggie's expression looked desperate as she studied me. "You need to call her. Text her. Something."

My stomach churned at her words. It made me feel uneasy. The news of Peter entering the race mixed with my relationship with the women of Magnolia had me drowning. I was swimming and swimming, and yet I couldn't reach the top of the water to catch my breath.

Was this how I died? What would my tombstone say? *Here lies Victoria. All she did was fail.*

I reached out and grabbed my water glass. I downed half before I felt clear-headed enough to face what Maggie was saying.

I wiped my lips with the cloth napkin under my utensils and turned to face her. She didn't look upset or angry, just worried. Was she worried about me or Clementine? After all, they were friends. What were we?

She reached out and rested her hand on mine. The

feeling of pressure startled me. I wanted to pull away, but I didn't know how. What was she doing?

"I'm saying something because I care. I care about you, and I care about Clementine."

I blinked as her words settled in my mind. She cared about me?

"Don't look so scared. I consider you a friend." She pulled her hand back to drum her fingers on the table. "I didn't know anyone when I came here, and now, I have a group of friends that I'm sure I could never live without. This town took me in and cared for me. The last thing I want is to see it torn apart." Her eyes glistened as she stared out the window.

A prickling sensation scratched my throat as my own emotions boiled up inside of me. She was right. There was something about this town and these people that pulled at my heart. It made me want to be a better person. It made me want to fight for it.

If Peter wanted to be mayor, he needed to prep for battle. This was my home. This was my town. And there was no way I was going to let it go.

Not without a fight.

Magnolia was mine.

SHARI

It felt cliché to say that I was finally happy, but I *was* finally happy. My mind was reeling from the evening I spent with Danny and the kiss we shared, and I never really came back down to reality. It had been a week since our date, and there was nothing I wanted more than to see him.

Feel him.

Kiss him.

I sighed as I leaned back in my chair and away from my desk. I bounced a few times as I tapped my pen on my desk while keeping my gaze trained on the office. I wanted to make up an excuse to go down to Danny's room and see him, but this was his first official week as Bella's teacher, and I didn't want to embarrass him. Or make him nervous.

So I forced myself to sit in my chair, waiting.

Waiting for the bell to ring. Waiting for the school to

clear. Waiting for my kids to be fed, bathed, and put to bed. Then I would text him. Maybe even call. Would he come over?

Was that the wrong thing to ask? Was it too soon? I knew in my head that I shouldn't be so quick to let a man back into my life. Not when my divorce papers were sitting in my dresser. Not when my kids were struggling.

I knew that the answer was to slow things down, so why hadn't the butterflies in my stomach gotten the memo? They seemed to be perfectly content, flitting around with no intention of ever leaving. At least, not when I was thinking about Danny. Which happened more that I cared to admit.

My cell phone rang. Desperate for the distraction, I picked it up and pressed it to my cheek before I even bothered to look and see who it was. It could be a spammer and I'd still take the call. Anything to take my mind off Danny and how much I wanted to see him again.

To make sure he was real and that I hadn't just made it all up in my head.

"Hello?" I asked as I tapped the end of my pen against the paper I'd been filling out.

"Shari?"

Like ice water poured down my back, the sound of Craig's voice caused my entire body to freeze. My limbs went still as I stared hard at the floor in front of my desk.

"Craig?" I asked. I hated how weak I sounded. I hated how he could cause this kind of reaction inside of me from one single word. I knew no matter what, he was going to forever be in my life, but it was going to take some time to get over what he did to me.

"Yeah."

Silence filled the air between us, and it was taking all of my strength not to hang up the phone. It was amazing how I could go from complete bliss to feeling as if all I could do was crawl inside of myself and die.

"I want to talk about tonight. I'm planning on getting the kids."

Anger pricked the back of my neck. He wanted to get the kids? Why? "Have you found a place?" My voice sounded strained, and I hated that it gave away how I felt. Why couldn't I be more calm and collected?

"I have. And I've furnished it too." He paused. "It's time I see them again, Shari. I'm still their father."

His words were like daggers in my chest. I knew he had a right to see them. But I hated that he'd never showed this kind of fight for us when we were with him. When we were standing right there, begging him to love us.

It took getting me out of his life for him to suddenly realize that his children mattered. How I had been so blind to his selfishness was beyond me. But it didn't matter. He was moving on, and so was I. We could be civil enough to speak to each other, but that was all. I could do that for my children.

"Let me ask them if they want to go with you, and I'll get back to you." I wanted some control of this situation. It was petty, I know, but I wanted to keep him waiting. He left. He cheated. He owed me. I started pulling my phone from my cheek when I heard his voice.

"Shari."

I hesitated. "What?"

"I want to see them."

Tears clung to my eyelids, and I closed my eyes for a moment in an effort to keep them at bay. I couldn't cry over Craig. Not anymore. I had to be stronger. "I know."

"Please let me come get them."

I squeezed my eyes. The angry part of me wanted to fight him. To tell him he'd hurt us and he should be punished. But I knew that wasn't right. Tag and Bella needed their father no matter how I felt about the man. If I loved my children, I would encourage them to see him.

"Fine. Be at the house at five to pick them up." I cleared my throat and gathered my strength. I could do this. I could be strong.

"Thanks," he said. His voice had a lighter hint to it. As if that was all he needed to hear.

I hated that he was happy. He shouldn't be happy. Not after he hurt me.

I said goodbye, and he said he would be there at five o'clock sharp. I didn't respond as I hung up the phone and blew out my breath. I tipped my head forward and rested it in the crook of my arm. If I was this exhausted after one five-minute conversation, what was seeing him going to do to me?

What was spending an entire weekend alone going to do to me?

I straightened and glanced around my desk. I was going to bury myself in work and pretend that five o'clock didn't exist. I just needed to take each hour one at a time. That was the only way I going to survive.

———

My entire body ached as I shut the front door behind me. I could still hear Craig's idling engine as he finished packing the kids' belongings into his car. His headlights shone in through the front window where I stood in the dark, waiting for him to leave. Waiting to break down like I'd wanted to do all day.

Bella was unsure how she felt about leaving with Craig, but Tag had been surprisingly chipper. He'd packed his things in record time and then proceeded to plop himself next to the door in anticipation.

I tried not to take offense at his actions. But it did hurt me that he was so lively when it came to seeing his father, yet so withdrawn when it came to me. I couldn't figure out why it was so easy for him to forgive his father but not me. I didn't want it to bother me, but it did. Deeply.

The headlights began to move, and I held my breath as I watched them disappear as Craig drove down the street.

Now completely alone, I collapsed on the floor, tears spilling from my eyes. I tipped my head forward and rested it on my knees. I felt as if someone was pulling my heart out of my chest, and I was bleeding out as a result.

I allowed myself to cry for only a few minutes before I

pulled myself up off the floor. I couldn't wallow forever. I was going to have to discover who Shari was without her kids. After all, this wasn't going to be the only time Craig came to pick them up. This was going to be a regular thing, and I needed to find a way to cope if I was going to survive. I couldn't react this way every time.

After washing my face and reapplying my makeup, I stared at my reflection in the mirror as anticipation rose up inside of me. There was no way I was going to spend this evening alone. And there was only one person I wanted to see.

I sent Danny a quick text.

Me: Can I see you tonight?

Butterflies filled my stomach as I awaited his response.

I had only been able to catch a glimpse of him today after school. He'd taken on Mrs. Davis' job as bus patrol and had been heading out with the group. I gave him a small wave, and his smile turned my knees to mush. He added a quick wink on top of that, and I melted.

I hoped all of that meant he wanted to see me again as well.

Danny: I thought you'd never ask. I'll be there in fifteen.

I couldn't stop the smile that spread across my lips as I read his text a few more times. Then I set my phone down and proceeded to try to pick out an outfit to wear. I wanted to look sexy. I didn't want to look like Shari the divorcée or Shari the mom. I wanted to look like…Shari.

I finally settled on a pair of dark skinny jeans and a

floral peplum top. I'd turned off my light and was headed out into the hallway when I heard his knock. My entire body lightened as heat flushed my skin. This was what I needed.

I hurried over to the door and pulled it open. Danny was standing on the other side with his arm propped up on the doorframe, which brought his face close to mine. It startled me for a moment, but one look into his dark, warm eyes, and I felt like I was home.

Like this was where I belonged.

"Hey," I breathed out.

His sexy half smile emerged, and the butterflies in my stomach sped up.

"Hey," he said as he straightened.

Silence engulfed us. I felt like I could stand here forever. Having him here helped me relax. With him next to me, I didn't have to think. I could just…be.

And I didn't want to think.

Action took over, and I reached out and fisted his leather jacket in my hands as I pulled him toward me. He chuckled and moved with me, allowing me to take control as I rose up onto my tiptoes and pressed my lips to his.

Warmth spread across my skin as we fell into the kiss. It was deeper and more passionate than it had been on the beach. Maybe it was my desperation to feel something other than sadness. I wanted to be happy. And Danny made me happy.

He bent down, and his arm swept my knees. With his other hand on my back, he pulled me up to his chest, never once breaking our kiss. I clung to his neck. I was worried if I let go, he would leave. And I couldn't have another man leave. Not when I felt this vulnerable.

Danny carried me over to the couch, where he sat down. I moved to straddle him as I parted my lips and allowed him in. I tangled my fingers in his hair as his hands moved from my lower back to my shoulders and then rested on either side of my face.

When he finally pulled away, I was out of breath. My whole body was pulsing with pleasure, and I was grateful for the reprieve from my thoughts that kissing him gave me. I slipped off his lap and onto the couch. I snaked my arm under his and found his hand. He threaded his fingers through mine and gave my hand a squeeze.

"That was quite a greeting," he said. His voice was low and husky, and I loved that I was able to cause a reaction in him like he caused in me.

I nodded as I rested my head on his shoulder. "I missed you."

He pulled back slightly, and I could tell that he was looking at me. I tipped my face up to meet his gaze. "Really?" he asked.

I nodded again. I felt so raw and vulnerable right now, but I trusted Danny. Despite what Craig did to me, I wanted to love again. And I could see myself doing that with Danny.

He leaned forward and brushed his lips against mine. Then he pulled back. "I missed you too. You know, it's hard being in the same building as you. I can't count the number of times I wanted to find you and pull you into one of those custodian closets."

Warmth filled my soul as I loosened my grip on his hand so I could trace my fingers against his palm. "That would be exciting," I whispered.

"Really?"

I nodded as I pushed off him so I could study him. "But inappropriate."

He raised his eyebrows as he wrapped his arm around my waist and pulled me into him. I had to rest my hands on either side of him, effectively caging him in. He tipped his gaze up to meet mine as my hair cascaded down around him.

"Well then, I guess we'll just have to wait until after work." He pushed himself up and kissed me again.

I giggled against his lips and then pulled back. "I guess we will."

We fell into another kiss, this one lasting much longer than any of the previous. But it felt so right. It was exactly what I needed. The broken pieces of my heart were finally beginning to mend. I still had a long way until I was whole, but this was a start.

And that was all I needed. A start.

17

VICTORIA

Things had gone from bad to worse. It was Friday, but it felt like a million years had passed from when I was at the inn talking to Maggie and meeting with Collin. What had started out as something positive had quickly turned sour, and I was no closer to feeling victorious despite my best efforts.

Peter had released the big guns. He'd bought up ads in the newspaper and the local news station. He was hosting a carnival this weekend, and it was all the town was talking about. Peter's name was on everyone's lips. As much as I wanted to run away from the hopelessness I felt, I couldn't. The stark reminder that I just might fail was staring me in the face, mocking me everywhere I went.

I pulled into the driveway just as I saw Danny speed out of the garage. I had to pull my car to the side so he could pass. He looked like a man on a mission. He was so distracted that he didn't even return my wave.

I sighed as I watched him pull out onto the street and disappear. Wherever he was going, he seemed determined to get there five minutes ago. I wanted to feel happy for him, I did, but I hated that he'd been gone more than he'd been around all week. I wanted to talk to him. To get his ideas. But between work and whatever he was doing in the evenings, he was barely home.

Which left me alone to wallow in my self-pity and to ward off Mom and Dad's disappointed gazes. They'd seen the polls. They'd heard the talk around town. They knew that I was losing. Even if I didn't want to admit it out loud, they knew. It was written across their faces.

I pulled into the garage and let my engine idle. I closed my eyes and rested my head against the seat. I took in a few deep breaths as hopelessness threatened to overcome me.

This was not how I saw this year going. This was not how I saw this reelection going. I'd deluded myself into thinking that my win could possibly be easy, but that had been a pipe dream that I was foolish enough to encourage.

Not wanting to look pathetic anymore, I gathered my things and climbed out of the car. After getting into the house, I shut the garage door and dropped my items on the floor. The house was quiet, and that made me feel happy for a moment. I wanted to be alone to wallow.

I padded into the kitchen and pulled out a bottle of wine. Just as I began to pour, Dad walked in. His presence sent shivers down my spine as I was greeted with his icy glare.

"Drinking?" he asked.

I continued pouring, ignoring the accusation in his tone. I returned the cork and then set the bottle in the fridge. When I turned around, Dad hadn't moved from his spot. He stood there with his arms folded across his chest and his perfect glower focused right on me.

"I think I've earned it," I said as I tipped the glass to my lips.

Dad moved closer to me. "You haven't earned it. Not until you are reelected. Then you drink." He was angry, which only fueled my own anger.

"I'm exhausted," I said, my voice breaking with that revelation. That was the truth. I was exhausted. Emotionally, physically, mentally. I was pretty sure that I didn't have the strength to do this anymore. This push to be perfect for him was crushing me.

"You can't afford to be exhausted." Dad reached out and pulled my wineglass from me. I growled, but he held his ground. "Go to the fair. Walk around. Talk to people. You can't let Peter beat you." The desperation in Dad's voice threw me off guard.

I blinked a few times as I studied him. He was worried, which only made me feel like crap. I didn't want to disappoint my parents despite how frustrated they made me. I wanted them to be happy like I wanted to be happy. But it didn't seem like I could have both. And if I were honest with myself, I was tired of choosing their happiness over mine.

"Aren't you tired?" I asked. Tears clung to my lids as I stared at Dad.

His expression only hardened. "You don't have time to be tired. You can be tired once you win." He leaned in closer to me. "And you haven't won yet."

I held his gaze as the intensity of his stare washed over me. He was determined to elicit a reaction from me, and normally it would have worked. Normally it would push me to do better. To work harder. But not now. For some reason, his determination to see me succeed just made me exhausted.

It made me want to rebel.

But before I could say anything, my phone rang. I pulled away from Dad and walked over to where I'd dropped my bags when I came in. After locating my phone, I brought it to my cheek.

"Hey, Sawyer. What's up?" I was ready for some good news, although I doubted Sawyer had any.

"Victoria?"

I nodded. "Yep."

Sawyer was silent for a moment. He had bad news and was trying to decide how to give it to me. My entire body felt like ice as I waited. I thought about asking him to hurry up, but I couldn't bring myself to. After all, I knew it was going to be bad. Why rush bad news?

"Collin's backing Peter. I just got the email."

My stomach sank like a rock. That whole ridiculous lunch had been for nothing. Sure, Collin had hinted that he was considering Peter, but I'd figured that was just talk. I didn't expect him to back someone else.

"Of course he is," I said as I collapsed on a barstool. Every muscle in my body ached from the stress I was carrying around.

"I just don't know what we can do to save this. We're hemorrhaging, and I fear it's gotten to the point where we can't survive."

He didn't have to say what I already knew. We were in trouble, and there was no way we were going to get out of it. There was no light at the end of this tunnel.

"Yeah," I whispered. I could feel Dad's stare, but I couldn't bring myself to meet it. He was going to tell me to fight, but the problem was I didn't have any fight left in me.

"We'll talk on Monday, but I think you need to figure out what your exit strategy will be." Sawyer sounded disappointed, and I hated that I'd caused that in him. He wasn't only my campaign manager, he was my friend. He put a lot of work into me, and I hated that I'd let him down.

"I'm sorry."

"It's not your fault, Victoria. These things happen."

Not to me. I never allowed things like this to happen. I wanted to stop it. I wanted to succeed. Even if politics didn't bring me happiness anymore, I was too stubborn to be beaten by someone else, especially when that someone was Peter Tippens.

But there was always going to come a point where I would fall and not be able to get up again. And I couldn't help but feel like this was that moment. How could I stop this? It was a rock rolling downhill and picking up speed. If I stood in front of it, I was going to get crushed, and I couldn't have that happen. I needed something to hang onto. Being beaten to a pulp would leave me broken and exposed.

And I couldn't survive if that happened.

I said goodbye to Sawyer and hung up. Dad was hovering by me as I set my phone down on the countertop and let out a sigh.

"What was that about? What did Sawyer say?"

Anger filled my gut as I glared at my father. He was so desperate to see me be the mayor once more that he didn't bother to ask me what was wrong. I was fairly certain that my emotions were written across my face. I knew I looked upset, and yet Dad chose to ignore that in favor of demanding that I tell him what was happening to my campaign.

"It doesn't matter," I said as I pushed away from the counter and stood. "It's over now."

I turned and headed down the hallway. Dad followed hot on my heels. He wasn't done with this conversation, even if I was.

"It's not over. Why is it over?" His hand reached out and wrapped around my elbow. "Victoria," he said. There was a clip to his voice that reminded me of my childhood. He was speaking to me like he did when I had been eight and washed his Jaguar with rocks.

Which made sense. That was how he saw me. I was a child to him. That was all. He was never going to see me as someone else. Someone strong. Someone grown-up.

"What do you want from me?" I asked, turning around to face him. I was tired, and I wanted him to see that. He was exhausting me. Why couldn't he just leave me alone?

I must have startled him because he stepped back with his eyes wide. His upper lip quivered as he stared at me. My breath was jagged, and my shoulders rose and fell as I stared at him.

"Victoria, I just want…" His voice trailed off as he studied me.

Guilt coated my body when I saw how confused he was. It was as if he wasn't sure how to read my reaction. I hated making my family feel uncomfortable. Even though they angered me, all I wanted was for them to feel happy. That's why I'd always done what they wanted. Why I'd become who they wanted me to be.

"What?" I asked again. This time I forced my voice to be calm. I couldn't lose my cool. Not like this.

Dad studied me and then sighed. "I just wanted you to succeed."

Tears clung to my eyelids. Why did success only mean one thing for my parents? Why did I have to carry on the family name in politics for them to see me as successful? I'd always gone along with being the person they wanted me to be. I'd never asked or doubted what they wanted. But I was never happy, and I was tired of not being happy.

"I'm going to go," I said as I sidestepped him and made

my way back into the kitchen. I grabbed my purse and hurried out to the garage. Dad didn't follow after me, which both angered me and relieved me at the same time. I didn't want to talk anymore about this, but I also wanted to feel like he cared about me and not just what I was giving up.

But I'd always learned to expect the least from my parents. Then I would never be disappointed. I never expected that he was going to come running after me, and as I pulled out of the driveway without Dad chasing after me, I wasn't disappointed.

Not even a little bit.

I drove around Magnolia for an hour before I found myself outside of the inn. It was dark out now, and the lights from the windows made the whole building shine. Maggie had decorated for Fall with pumpkins, gourds, and straw. It looked so homey—more so than my own home. And right now, that was what I needed.

A place that felt warm and welcoming.

I parked and got out. I'd eat dinner and relax in the dining room until Maggie kicked me out. Or, if I was obstinate enough, I'd grab a room and stay the night. I slammed the driver's door and pulled out my phone. I didn't want to be alone tonight, and if Danny wasn't busy, I wanted his company.

So I shot my brother a quick text telling him where I was and asking him to meet me when he was done doing whatever he was doing. The smell of the salty breeze mixed with the sound of waves had a healing effect on me.

When I pulled open the front door and felt the warmth and chatter of everyone inside, my entire body began to relax. I stepped inside the inn and took a deep breath. This was where I belonged for the night. Here, I didn't have to worry about the election or disappointing my family.

I could be just me.

After searching around for Maggie and coming up empty, I made my way into the dining room. It was busy, with people sitting at the tables talking and laughing, but there was no Maggie among them. Remembering her in an apron the other day, I wondered if she was in the kitchen.

I was pretty certain that I was breaking a few rules, but that had never stopped me before. So I pushed through the swinging door and into the large kitchen. All sorts of smells greeted me. Whatever the chef was preparing for dinner, it smelled amazing. I glanced around and took in the large bowls of mashed potatoes, a roast sitting on a platter, and gravy bubbling on the stove.

This was never how my house felt growing up. We always either hired a chef, or Mom would order out. My house never felt this homey or cozy.

"Coming through," a deep voice said from behind me.

I yelped and turned just in time to see Brett emerge from the back room with a sheet full of raw cookie dough. My cheeks heated as his gaze raked over me, but he didn't stop to talk. He made his way over to one of the two ovens on the far wall and slipped the cookie sheet into it.

With the oven door closed, he turned to face me. "What brings you in here?" he asked as he wiped his hands on his apron. His half smile was endearing as he studied me.

I hated how flustered I felt under his gaze. There was something about him that was drawing me in, and it made me feel even more out of control. I shouldn't be intrigued by this stranger. Not when my life was crumbling around me.

"I was looking for Maggie," I said, hating how my voice sounded weak. I needed to get a grip on my emotions before they exposed me.

Brett glanced around. "She's not in here."

I nodded. "I got that."

"Anything I can help you with?" He leaned forward. I knew that he was being nice, but all that made me want to do was leave. Run far away to a place where I could hide from all of my failures.

"No. I'll just keep looking for her." I hurried to leave.

From the corner of my eye, I saw Brett part his lips to respond, but I didn't let him. There was no way I wanted to stand there and continue our conversation. If I did, it was only a matter of time until he would discover how much of a failure I was. And I wasn't ready for that. Let him believe I was strong for a bit longer. Then, reality could come crashing down around me.

Once I was back out in the dining room, I felt like I could breathe. I leaned against the wall and focused on calming my mind. I didn't like how I felt around him or the fact that I was as discombobulated as I was.

I scanned the room and stopped when Danny's face appeared in my line of sight. I furrowed my brow as I studied him. He was seated at a table with a woman. Was he here on a date? Who was he with?

The woman had her back to me, but I could tell that Danny liked her. He was leaning in, and when I took a step to the side, I saw that he was resting their entwined hands on his lap. They were trying to be discrete, but I could tell what was happening.

Since when did he start dating someone? And why didn't he tell me?

I started in their direction. I wanted to know who this woman was that would cause him to abandon me to deal with our parents alone. Just as I neared his table, I stopped dead in my tracks.

Shari?

They were chatting and didn't notice my approach. But just before I could slip away, Shari's gaze met mine and her face turned paper-white. Her eyes widened, and I could tell from the way her arm dropped to her side that she'd pulled her hand back.

"Victoria," she squeaked out.

Danny hadn't noticed me, but when Shari announced my presence, he glanced over and gave me a wide smile. "Hey, sis." Then he glanced around. "What are you doing here?"

I cleared my throat, completely thrown not only from

my interaction with Brett, but by seeing my brother date a woman who was the same age as me. And divorced. Did he not know what he was getting into? "I was going to ask the same thing," I managed out. Thankfully, I sounded stronger than I felt, which was allowing me to save face.

"We're eating dinner," Danny said as if there was nothing wrong with what was going on in front of me.

"Like a date?" I asked. I couldn't quite understand why I was so angry about this. If it were any other time in my life, I honestly wouldn't have cared. But I was breaking, and the only person in my life that I could depend on was off on a date with my friend—or someone who I'd convinced myself was my friend.

Danny nodded. "Yeah. Like a date."

My entire body was shaking now, and the last thing I wanted to do was have a breakdown in front of these two. I needed to get out of here. Right now.

I didn't respond as I stumbled from the dining room and took off to the front door. This place was supposed to be a haven of comfort for me, and yet, my brother and Shari had managed to rip that out from under me.

I was officially alone. I had no friends and no family.

I had nothing.

"Tori!"

I could hear Danny call after me, but I didn't stop. Instead, I ran to my car and climbed in. The gravel spewed from under my tires as I peeled out of the parking lot and down the road. Darkness surrounded me as I drove.

Tears streamed down my cheeks as I contemplated not

going home. I thought about just driving until I couldn't drive anymore. After all, what did I have here?

My parents were disappointed in me. My brother was busy dating my friend. And my town?

Well, they'd abandoned me and everything I'd given them the moment a Tippens ran for mayor.

I had nothing. I was officially town-less.

I was officially alone.

18

SHARI

I recognized the look on Victoria's face. It was the look of betrayal. Something was going on with her, and I couldn't help but feel responsible for her pain. I swallowed as I watched Danny return to the table. His eyebrows were knit together, and his hands were shoved into his front pockets.

He was just as concerned as I was.

"She okay?" I asked as I took a sip of my water.

Danny blew out his breath. He shrugged and took a bite of the roast that had been delivered while he was gone. "I think so. She's going through some stuff." He chewed thoughtfully and then glanced over at me. "But I never expected her to react like that to us." He pushed around some of his mashed potatoes.

"That was strange, huh?" I'd never expected her to get mad that Danny and I were dating. I mean, we were both adults, and it wasn't like Victoria and I were that close.

The book club was the first time we'd talked since high school.

My stomach was too knotted to eat, so I focused on sipping my water. "Should we do something?"

Danny scooped up a mound of his potatoes and slipped them into his mouth. "Like what?"

"I don't know. Follow her?"

Danny shook his head as he swallowed. "Bad idea. It's best to let her work through these things alone first." He shivered. "She can get violent."

I swatted his arm. He feigned pain as he moved to avoid me.

"Hey, I'm just the messenger."

"I'm sure she's not the same as she was growing up."

He snorted and sipped his beer. "I wish I could say she's changed. But that woman is stubborn."

I nodded in agreement. "Yeah. She got mad at Clementine last week."

"Clementine? Why?"

I sighed. "She's starting a dance studio and installed poles for a pole dancing class."

Danny sat up in his seat. Then his gaze raked over me, and my entire body flushed. "Pole dancing? Really?" He leaned in to me, his voice turning husky. "Are you signing up?"

His reaction had me blushing uncontrollably. I wanted to convince myself that he was just being nice, but when my gaze met his and I saw the desire there, I knew there was something more.

He wanted me in a way that a man hadn't wanted me in a long time. And that both thrilled and frightened me. What if I disappointed him? He was used to dainty, thin girls. I was a mom. I had stretch marks and fat I couldn't quite get rid of.

Suddenly, he pressed his lips to my neck, and I startled. "You're beautiful. And sexy. And everything a man wants." He gave me a wink as he returned to his food.

I sat there, stunned. Had he just said those words to me?

"You looked like you were going to start spiraling. I wanted to stop it before you pulled away from me." Danny took a bite of his roast and gave me a wide smile.

I'd lost all train of thought, and I completely forgot how to form words in response. He looked satisfied that he'd sufficiently distracted me as he polished off his plate. I wanted to bring the conversation back to Victoria, but I was beginning to realize that we both needed to talk to her separately. If I wanted to heal my relationship with her, I was going to have to do it on my own.

If I tried to address it with Danny, he would just tell me to let it go again. That she'd come around. But I knew a lot about Victoria. She didn't just come around to anything.

I was going to have to talk to her and get her to open up. Which was easier said than done.

We finished dinner and paid. Maggie and I spoke for a few minutes, and I let her know what had happened with Victoria. She looked as concerned as I felt and promised talk to the other book club ladies to come up with a plan.

Danny and I spent the next hour outside of the inn, cuddled up next to each other in front of the bonfire that Archer was stoking as he and Danny talked.

I was more than happy to sit and listen to their conversation. They reminisced about the places in Europe they'd both seen. The more I listened to the life Danny had led before he came here, the more I began to realize that I didn't know much about him. He'd lived a life I could only dream of.

I had children and responsibilities. I couldn't just pack up one day and go off to some enchanting country and spend a few months there. And yet, that seemed to be Danny's M.O. before he came home.

That got me wondering—was he going to be happy to be tied down here? How long would he want to stay in Magnolia? Would he resent me for holding him back? Was I a fool to ask him to stay?

My thoughts weighed on my mind as I adjusted my seat. Danny must have noticed my hesitation because he tightened his arm around my shoulders and pulled me in closer. He paused in his conversation to plant a kiss on my head.

It made me feel better for a short moment, but it didn't remove the truth that was pricking me at the back of my mind. The truth that I was going to have to face sooner or later.

Danny and I were not meant for anything more than what we were doing now.

And that pain clung to me no matter how much I wanted to stay away from it.

"You okay?" Danny whispered into my hair as he turned his attention to me. Archer had been summoned by Maggie and excused himself, leaving Danny and I alone.

I nodded but kept my lips pinched together. I worried if I parted my lips the truth would be revealed. And I wasn't ready for the truth to come out.

"Do you want me to take you home?" He pulled back to glance down at me.

I kept my gaze focused on my hands as I nodded again. "Yeah. That would be good."

Danny paused, and I waited for him to say something, but he never did. Instead he just nodded and stood, extending his hand for me to take. I slipped my fingers in his, and he pulled me to my feet. The movement was so fast that it caught me off guard, and I was flung into his chest. He wrapped his arms around me and squeezed.

"We'll be just fine," he whispered when his lips found my ear.

I nodded but kept my arms tucked into my sides. He could say that, but I knew the truth. If I couldn't even convince Craig to stick around, how was I going to convince this global nomad to stay? I was a shadow of a person, and one day, Danny was going to wake up and see it.

I wasn't the person he wanted to settle down with. The stress of dealing with Craig and my children was going to be too much.

We were quiet as Danny drove me home. I kept my hands tightly gripped in my lap and my gaze turned outward. It was dark, and I could hardly see anything, but the stress of discussing our future was too much. There was no way I could face Danny with my fears and come away intact. So I preferred to ignore them until the very last minute.

He pulled into my driveway and idled the engine. I could see him glance over at me every few seconds as if he wanted to speak but wasn't sure what to say. And I wasn't sure he could say anything.

"I'll walk you to the door," he whispered as he unbuckled and opened his door.

I moved to protest, but he was outside before I could stop him. I watched as he rounded the hood of the car and made his way to my door. The release engaged, and the cool night air washed over me as he extended his hand to help me out.

I obliged, and soon, we were standing side by side outside of his car. He shut the door and turned to focus on me. He looked confused as he stared down at me. I knew he wanted to ask me what was wrong, but I was secretly hoping he'd just let it go.

"Did I do something?" he asked.

My heart broke at his words. I wanted to tell him that he was perfect; I was the one who was tainted. But I knew he'd try to defend me. He would say he didn't care that I was divorced or that I had kids. I knew he'd try to convince me that none of that mattered. Which might be true for now. But eventually, it would matter.

And I didn't want to be around when that realization dawned on him.

"I just think we're fooling ourselves," I said slowly.

His eyebrows rose with each word. After I finished speaking, he blew out his breath and shoved his hands into his front pockets. He leaned back on his car as if I'd just punched him in the gut.

"Fooling ourselves? I'm not confused." His gaze met mine, and I could feel his intensity. He wanted me to feel the weight of his words. He wanted me to believe him.

And I wanted to. I really did. But at some point, one of us was going to need to face reality. It was a balance that was eventually going to come due.

"Danny, I just know how this will end."

Danny scoffed. "Because of your prick ex?" He straightened and moved until he was standing centimeters from me. He stared down at me so hard that I couldn't raise my gaze to meet his. I feared what I would find there. I needed as much strength as I could to walk away, and one look from him would crumble my will.

"This is not about Craig. This is about us and the fact that we are not forever." The words were a whisper as they escaped my lips. I wanted to give in and kiss him. To let go of the pain I was feeling and finally live, but I knew I couldn't.

"Please," Danny begged as he reached up and cradled my cheek. He leaned forward and brushed his lips against mine.

He was so gentle and so desperate that it caused the tears that I had been holding back to slip down my cheeks. I allowed my lips to linger with his. It was selfish, but I wanted to experience this moment for a bit longer. I wanted him next to me for a few seconds more before I pulled back and walked away forever.

"Mom?"

My entire body froze. My eyes whipped open, and I leapt back from Danny like I had been burned. I turned to see Tag standing there with his overnight bag slung over his shoulder and his eyes as wide as saucers.

Bella was standing behind him with her eyebrows knit together. She was squeezing her teddy bear and worrying her lips as she swept her gaze from me to Danny.

Craig was walking across the grass and had an equally confused expression on his face.

"Hey," I said in a loud and completely fake tone. "Hey, guys." My second attempt didn't sound any better. I was desperate to pull back from what had just happened. From the fact that my kids had now seen me kissing Danny. In a few minutes, he would pull out of the driveway and out of my life forever, so it wasn't going to matter.

But right now, they looked confused and hurt, and that was killing me.

"Let's go in the house and let your mom finish what she was doing," Craig said as he wrapped his arms around

Bella and Tag's shoulders and started steering them toward the front door.

I glared at him. I could tell he was enjoying this. And that irked me. At least, I'd waited until I was divorced to kiss someone else. He'd chosen to do that when we were supposed to be committed to each other.

He had no right to feel smug about any of this.

Once they disappeared into the house, I went into problem-solving mode. I turned to Danny and offered him a weak yet apologetic smile. "I think you should go," I said.

Danny looked just as broken as he had a few minutes ago. Back before the kids walked up on us.

"Please—"

"I can't." The words came out fast. I knew I wasn't going to be able to remain strong if he asked, and right now, I needed to be strong. There were going to be repercussions from what Tag and Bella had witnessed. Plus, I knew I was going to have to deal with Victoria at some point.

Danny and I were fools if we thought we could just have a relationship and that would be it. That we weren't going to have to face reality eventually. We just got there faster than most. We weren't meant to be together. We were just a stop for each other on our road to discovering who we were and who we wanted.

Danny took a step back. I hated seeing his face contorted in pain. If I could, I would take it all away. But I couldn't. I couldn't say the things he wanted me to say. I couldn't be the person he needed me to be.

"Goodbye, Danny," I said as I wrapped my arms around my chest and took a few steps back. My heart was breaking, and I feared if I lingered, I would throw my resolve out the window and go running back to him.

But the thing that I've learned about pain is that it doesn't last forever. Every minute, every day, every week that you continue living after your heart has been broken, you get stronger. You get more resilient.

And from this last year, with everything I'd gone through with Craig, I'd learned I was stronger than I thought.

Gathering my courage, I turned and hurried across the lawn and up to my front stoop before I could change my mind. I opened the front door and slipped inside. After shutting the door, I leaned against it and let out the breath I'd been holding.

My heart felt as if a vice were surrounding it, squeezing it. I wanted to collapse on the ground and let the tears flow. I wanted to crawl under my covers and wallow in my self-pity.

But I couldn't. I had two very confused children to deal with.

I summoned what strength I had left and pushed off the door. I found my children in the living room, looking confused as they sat on the couch. Craig was in the armchair off to the side with his phone out. He was staring at the screen with an incredibly smug look on his face.

Great. He was not what I needed right now.

"Hey, guys," I said, hating the fake, chipper voice I was using, but what else did I have? I wasn't happy at all. But I didn't want my children to think I was upset with them. "What happened? I thought you were going to spend the weekend with Daddy."

I glanced at Craig. He shrugged but continued scrolling on his phone. "They decided they wanted to come home." Craig sighed as he set his phone down and moved to sit up. "What could I do?"

I stared at him. What kind of response was that? He was their father. He should fight for them more. "What happened?"

Bella was the first to look at me. Her big, brown eyes were full of tears as she leaned in and wrapped her arms around me. "I was scared you were lonely." She sobbed into my shirt. I pulled her close and squeezed her hard.

My already broken heart was hemorrhaging right now. My children were so lost. So confused. And it broke my heart.

"Tag?" I whispered as I glanced over at him.

His lips were pulled into a tight line, and he was picking at the fabric of his sweatshirt. He let out a *harrumph* as he shifted in his seat. "I missed my games," he muttered. I could tell he was trying to be tough, but there was something more to his expression. One that he was having a hard time hiding.

I reached over and pulled him into a hug. He was stiff about it but eventually allowed me to get closer to him. I sat there, holding both of my babies. Tears began to flow as I let myself feel the pain I'd been trying to keep at bay for so long.

The pain of the divorce. The pain of being a single mother. And the pain of trying to discover who I was without hurting those that I loved.

A few minutes passed before I felt strong enough to face what I needed to say to them. I knew they were scared about what the divorce between Craig and I meant, but that didn't mean that their father was a bad guy. Eventually, they were going to be okay.

I pulled back, so I could focus on both of them. Bella's nose was running, and she kept wiping it with her sleeve. Tag's normally stony expression had cracked, and I could finally see my son peeking out from behind it.

"Listen," I said as I crouched down on the ground. "Things are new and they are scary right now. But your father and I will always be here for you." I glanced over at Craig, who was leaning forward and resting his elbows on his knees. "We may be getting a divorce, but we will always be your parents. Being with Dad doesn't hurt me. I want you to spend time with him and enjoy yourself."

I gave them both a big smile. This time, it wasn't fake. I meant it. All of it.

"It will take time to get used to it, but that's okay. We're all trying to get used to our new normal." I reached up and cradled Bella's cheek. She leaned into it as a look of relief fell over her face. "So what do you say? Want to give spending the weekend with Dad another shot?"

I glanced between Bella and Tag. They were quiet, and I could tell they were mulling over my words. Bella was the first to react. She gave me a wide, toothless grin and nodded. "I can go with Daddy."

I smiled as I pulled her into a hug. Then I glanced over at Tag. He looked conflicted but finally sighed. "I can, too."

I wrapped my other arm around Tag and squeezed. It felt like I was hugging a limp fish, but he wasn't pulling away. This was progress.

We gathered the kids' belongings and moved to the front door. When they were packed into the car, I turned to face Craig. I gave him an annoyed look. It irritated me how quickly he'd given up. I'd gotten over how quickly he gave up on our marriage. But he couldn't do this with our kids. Not now.

"Try harder next time," I said as I folded my arms across my chest and glared at him.

He sighed and scrubbed his hands over his face. "I tried. But they were adamant that they needed to come check on you." He let his hands fall. I didn't like the look he was casting my direction, but I didn't falter in my stance.

"New boyfriend?" he asked as he nodded to where Danny had been parked.

I narrowed my eyes as I set my jaw. "Good night, Craig." I hadn't had time to process what had happened, and there was no way I was going to attempt to work through it while standing in front of my ex.

"I was just wondering," he said as he held up his hands. Thankfully, he didn't push it further. Instead, he walked over to the driver's side and climbed in.

I waited on the front stoop until Craig was out of sight. I waved until Bella could no longer see me.

Now alone, I slipped into my house and stood in the entryway, in the dark.

Without my children or Craig around me, I let my tears fall.

My broken heart came to the forefront, and there was nothing keeping me from feeling the pain that came from walking away.

Danny and I were finished, and it was going to take me a long time to get over it.

I may be stronger than I'd thought, but that didn't mean that I was unbreakable.

I had broken into a million pieces. And I feared I was never going to be whole again.

19

VICTORIA

The next week went from bad to worse, and there was nothing I could do to stop it. Sawyer tried. I tried. But the polls kept tipping in Peter's favor, and it was getting to the point that my campaign was beyond repair.

I knew it. Sawyer knew it. Mom and Dad knew it. Every time we were in the same room, they were quiet, and I could feel their stares and unspoken words. To them, I was a failure, and it was eating me alive.

Danny was no help. It had been a week since I'd seen him at the inn with Shari, and ever since he came home that night, he'd been either working or moping. He'd come home and cement himself to the couch. He was upset about something, but I wasn't in the headspace to figure out what.

I was relieved when I woke up on Saturday morning. The sun was streaming into my room, so I pulled my covers up over my head and reveled in the darkness. I didn't have to go into the office today, and I'd told Sawyer to cancel all of my appearances. I didn't want to admit defeat, but I also didn't want to continue when there was no point.

I was flip-flopping and figured it would be better if I just ignored the things that were causing me pain rather than facing them. At least for today.

I stretched out on my bed. The feeling of stress leaving my body helped me to relax. I was going to spend the day doing what *I* wanted to do. I was going to wallow in my self-pity until I felt better.

I was determined to make this day all about me.

By ten o'clock, I'd watched a chick flick on Netflix and eaten the stash of chocolate I had hidden in my nightstand. I was feeling pretty good. I had my phone out and was getting ready to order some Chinese food for delivery when there was a soft knock on the door.

I paused the movie and glanced over. I wanted to tell whoever it was to go away. By my calculations, it was either Mom, Dad, or Danny. And right now, I was not interested in talking to any of them.

I figured that silence was the best way to deal with unwanted guests, so I pulled my covers over my head, planning to hide until they went away. My entire body tensed when I heard the door click open and someone entered my room.

Frustrated, I pulled the covers off my head and sat up. "What do you want?" I asked. I didn't attempt to soften my tone. Instead, I unleashed the full Victoria Holt. My glare halted when it met not my family, but Maggie. She was standing in the middle of my room with a sheepish look on her face.

"Maggie?" I asked as I blinked a few times, just to make sure I wasn't seeing things.

"Hey, Victoria. Sorry for barging in like this." She glanced around. "Your mom said I could come up here and if you didn't answer, to just come in."

I collapsed against my pillows. Typical. Mom wasn't good at confrontation, so Maggie being here meant she could pass that responsibility off onto someone else. I allowed my arms to fall to my side, where I found my remote and turned the show back on. "You can join me if you want," I said, motioning toward the spot next to me.

Maggie hesitated but walked over. After kicking off her shoes, she climbed up onto the bed. We sat in silence, watching the movie until I couldn't take it anymore. I clicked the TV off and turned to face her.

"Why are you here?" I asked.

Maggie turned to face me. She looked worried as her gaze roamed over me. "We are worried about you."

I frowned. "We?"

"Me, Fiona, Clementine…Shari."

I shook my head at the mention of Shari. I wasn't quite ready to face what I had seen last week. It wasn't so much that they were dating—Danny dated a lot of girls—it had more to do with the fact that I was struggling, and my friend and brother weren't there to help. I knew it sounded selfish, but I needed them.

"I'm sure you are overexaggerating," I said as I pulled up a throw pillow and hugged it.

Maggie shook her head. "I'm not. The ladies are really worried about you. We've called an emergency book club meeting."

My gaze shifted to a book on my shelf. The one we'd decided to read this month. I hadn't even cracked open the cover. "Well, you'll have to do it without me. I haven't even started it."

"It's not that kind of meeting." She swung her legs over the side of the bed and stood. Then she straightened her shirt and nodded toward my bathroom. "Get showered and dressed. I'll be downstairs waiting for you."

I parted my lips to protest, but Maggie didn't look as if she was going to entertain anything I had to say. She marched over to my door and left before I could respond.

Now alone, I stared at the black screen of the TV. I wanted to make an excuse as to why I couldn't go. There was no way I wanted to participate in whatever they had planned for me. It would get in the way of the pity party that I was throwing right now.

My phone chimed, so I grabbed it off of my nightstand and swiped it on.

Maggie: Seriously not leaving until you come down here.

I growled as I set my phone back down and pulled my covers from my body. Fine. If she wanted this, then I'd play along. That didn't mean I was going to enjoy it, and it definitely didn't mean I was going to get anything out of it. I'd listen to what the ladies said, and then I would come home and hide in my bed once more.

I settled on jeans and a t-shirt once I was showered and dried off. I threw my hair up into a messy bun and applied minimal makeup. Once I was dressed, I slipped on my tennis shoes and headed out of my room.

Maggie was sitting at the counter when I walked into the kitchen. She had a cup of coffee in front of her, and she was munching on a biscotti. I could tell by the spread that Mom had been down here recently. I walked over to the fridge and opened it to grab a water bottle.

When I turned back around, I saw that Maggie had stood up. She looked confused as her gaze swept over me.

"What?" I asked and then winced at my tone. I hadn't meant to sound harsh. I was just exhausted.

Maggie didn't seem fazed. Instead, she just chuckled as she shook her head. "Nothing. It's just…" She wiggled her finger in my direction. "I've never seen you look so casual before."

I glanced down at my clothes and then back up to her. She had a point. I was normally in business suits and heels. In fact, I doubted she'd ever seen me in everyday clothes before.

"I wear t-shirts and jeans." I shrugged and brought the water to my lips.

Maggie snorted. "Right."

I gave her an exasperated look, but she just shrugged. "Are you ready?"

I took in a deep breath and nodded. "Yeah. I am." I grabbed my purse from the nearby hook and slung it over my shoulder. Then I motioned toward the front door. "Let's get this over with."

I felt like a prisoner being marched off to the gallows. There was so much of this that I wanted to avoid, but I knew even if I backed out now, I was going to have to face Maggie and the other book club ladies eventually. I might as well rip off the bandage and do it all now. Then, they couldn't force me into something like this again. I could live happily alone, and no one would bother me again.

The ride to Clementine's dance studio was short. I kind of wished Maggie had warned me about where we were going before I'd agreed to get into the car with her. When she parked alongside the building and gave me a huge grin, I knew that there was no way I was getting out of this.

I might as well put on my big-girl panties and get out of the car.

I followed behind Maggie as we walked into the dance studio. Set up in the middle of the floor was a table full of all sorts of breakfast items. Pastries, eggs, french toast. All of it made my mouth water and my stomach churn. Apparently eating half a pound of chocolate on an empty stomach wasn't such a good idea.

I raised my eyebrows as I glanced around the room. Maggie had moved off to the side next to Clementine.

Fiona was standing in the corner with her son, Alex, balanced on her hip. Her mother, Anna, was next to her. Brenda, the owner of Shakes, was also there along with a few more people from town.

They were all smiling at me in a way that made me feel uncomfortable. Why were they being so nice to me? Was it because they pitied me? Was I that pathetic?

"What's going on?" I asked, dragging out every syllable.

"It's a party for you," Brett's deep voice said from behind me. I turned to see him standing there with a tray of cut-up fruit balanced on his shoulder. He gave me a wide smile and a wink as he passed me and set the food down on the table.

My stomach was in knots as I glanced around the room once more. Was this really for me? Tears clung to my lids despite my efforts to keep them at bay. I wanted to remain strong, but I was so tired and so exhausted that I wasn't sure I had the strength to remain composed.

"We love you, Victoria," Fiona said as she handed her son off to her mom and walked over to me. She wrapped her arms around me and pulled me into a hug.

That removed the dam that was keeping my emotions at bay. Tears began to stream down my cheeks as I clung to Fiona. I was so tired of being someone I thought everyone wanted me to be. I was tired of feeling like a failure. I was tired of pretending to be strong when I felt so weak.

There was a silent hush that fell around the room, and suddenly, I was being hugged on all sides. Everyone was murmuring how much they loved and appreciated me—which only made me cry even more.

By the time they all let me go, I was a blubbering mess. I wiped at my cheeks and nose as I glanced around the room. A napkin appeared next to me, and I glanced over to see that Brett had been the one to produce it. He smiled, and I felt only more embarrassed.

I took the napkin quickly and blotted my nose. Then I focused on the group of women who surrounded me. I found Clementine in the crowd. She was keeping her distance but still making an effort to show her support.

I approached her. I knew I'd been wrong. I should have never snapped at her like I did. I wanted to make it better. We were close—well, as close as I get to people. I didn't want to lose her friendship.

"I'm sorry," I said as soon as I was standing in front of her.

Clementine's eyes widened as she studied me. I gave her a smile, one that didn't feel fake. It was the first time I wasn't pulling out my political smile, and instead, I was just being me. And that felt incredible.

She paused for a moment before she smiled. "It's fine, Victoria. I know you were stressed. It's not a big deal." She reached forward and gave me a quick hug.

I felt relieved that she wasn't angry at me any longer. But I knew I needed to do something else to really show how sorry I was. "I'll come to your classes," I blurted out.

Clementine glanced at me. "It's really okay."

I shook my head. "No, I'm going to come. It'll be good for me."

She hesitated and then nodded. "I look forward to you being there." Her smile was softer now, and I felt more relaxed.

This new Victoria was someone I could get behind. I felt...freer. Like this was who I was meant to be all along —even if I didn't know who *this* person was, yet. It felt exciting to discover her.

I spent the afternoon eating and talking. After my tears had dried, I felt more normal, more human. I felt happy for the first time in a long time.

Maggie was kind enough to drive me home, and when I got out of the car and stared up at the huge house in front of me, I realized what I needed to do. If I was going to change my life, if I was really going to be happy for the first time since I could remember, I needed to stand up for what I wanted and not what my parents or this town expected.

By the time I got inside the house, my confidence was floundering, but I pushed my fears aside. I found my parents sitting at the table, eating a late lunch. They weren't talking. Mom was on her phone, and Dad was reading the newspaper.

I entered the room, but neither looked up to acknowledge me.

So I spoke. "I'm pulling out of the election," I said in a blur of words.

Dad stopped chewing, and Mom glanced up at me. Her eyes were wide.

"You're what?" Dad finally asked after he choked down the food he was eating.

"I'm pulling out of the election. The polls don't look good for me, and I"—I took in a deep breath—"am not happy."

Dad bunched up the newspaper he was reading and threw it down onto the ground. Mom blubbered on about all the work they did to get me where I was. I could tell Dad was gearing up for some lecture, but I wasn't interested. In fact, I was done living under the cloud of my parents' expectations. So I turned and walked away.

Just before I was out of earshot, I threw, "And I'm moving out," over my shoulder.

I was shaking by the time I got into my room and shut the door. I collapsed on my bed as fear coursed through my veins at the speed of my racing heart. I buried my face into my covers as I tried to calm my body.

I was terrified, but I also felt...free. And that was amazing.

Once I was calm, I climbed off my bed and went searching for Danny. Something was up with him, and I was going to figure out what. There was no point in finding my own happiness when my kid brother looked like someone had yanked away his. He was a happy-go-lucky guy, so for him to be moping around like this was concerning.

It didn't take long for me to find him. He was in his

room on his bed with the drapes closed. His head was buried underneath his pillow. I flopped down on his bed and patted his shoulder.

He growled.

"Well, at least I know you are still alive," I said as I peered down at him.

"Go away."

I sighed, leaning against the headboard. "I quit. I'm not running for mayor. And I'm moving out. Want to come with me?" I glanced down to see if that piqued his interest.

I felt triumphant when he began to stir and then emerged from his covers. He pushed up until he was sitting next to me with his back against the headboard. He didn't speak right away. Something was wrong, and I felt like a horrible sister for not being there for him.

"This is a new side of you," he finally said.

I nodded. "I thought I'd take a page out of your *I don't care* book." I glanced over at him, and my heart hurt at how broken he looked. "What's wrong?" I asked before I could filter myself.

Danny sniffed but then shook his head. "It's nothing. At least, it's nothing I can fix."

I furrowed my brow and moved until I was facing him. "I don't believe that. You can fix anything. You're Danny Holt."

He scoffed and glanced over at me. His skin was pale, and his eyes bloodshot. He looked…miserable.

"Is it Shari? Did something happen there? And why didn't you tell me you two were dating?" I swatted his arm, hoping to lighten the mood, but it fell flat. So I sighed. "You gotta talk to me. I want to help."

Danny shook his head. "There's nothing you can do. It was over before it started. She said it's too hard." His voice slipped down to a whisper as he dropped his gaze. He took in a deep breath, and I couldn't help but picture Eeyore as he sat there.

My kid brother was hurting, and I knew what that was like. To want something but to realize that it might never happen. Which was ridiculous. I saw how she was smiling when she was around him.

"You can't give up. I saw the way she looked at you. In all the years she was with Craig, I never saw that same look in her eye." I punched his shoulder, hoping that would wake him up.

Danny pulled away. "Stop hitting me," he said, but the playful hint to his voice had returned.

I narrowed my eyes and forced the best mayoral voice I could. He needed to know that I was serious. "Do you like her?"

He studied me and then slowly nodded. "Yes."

"Do you want to get to know her more?"

"Yes."

Then I shrugged and climbed off his bed. I stood in front of him and nodded. "Then let's go get her."

20

SHARI

I was trying to move on, and I wanted to say I was being successful at it. But when it was quiet, or when I stopped moving and just sat, that's when the wave of regret would wash over me, and I would feel as if I couldn't breathe. I stretched out in my bed on Sunday, a full week since I'd told Danny to leave and not come back, and sucked in my breath as I stared up at the early morning light that crept across the ceiling.

The weight of regret bore down on me as Danny's face floated into my mind. I closed my eyes to allow myself to linger on his eyes, his nose, and his lips. My heart picked up speed, causing me to push that image out. After all, I knew what that response meant. I wasn't over him. Not even close.

"Mommy?" Bella's cautious voice asked.

I pushed to sitting as I glanced in the direction of my door. Bella was peeking between the doorframe and the door. Her eyes were wide, and her hair was disheveled from sleep. I gave her a wide grin and waved for her to join me. Her smile grew as she pushed open the door, sprinted across my floor, and leapt into bed.

"How did you sleep?" I asked as I wrapped my arm around her, and we snuggled down into the pillows and comforter.

Bella let out a loud yawn and then giggled. "Good."

I bent my wrist so I could start running my fingers through her hair. I stared over at her and decided to revel in the feeling of her next to me. I had Bella. I had Tag. I had my home and my job. Sure, I didn't have Danny, but that was okay. I had what I needed, and I was going to learn to be happy with that.

Bella found my remote and clicked on the TV. Soon, the sound of some cartoon washed through the room. I settled back against my pillows and closed my eyes. Sleep started taking over until I felt Bella shift next to me. It felt as if she were hovering over me, so I cracked open my eyes to see her right above me, looking down.

"Bella," I said, as I moved to get out from under her, "what are you doing?"

Bella looked sheepish as she moved to sit next to me. "Why were you kissing Mr. Holt?"

I nearly choked on my tongue at her question. Regret washed over me. So she'd not only seen me kissing Danny, but she also remembered it. Great.

I cleared my throat. "Well…" What did I say to that? I kissed him because I wanted to? Because I liked him? I inwardly groaned. I should have prepared more for this. If I was going to attempt dating again, I needed to have blanket responses to questions like this.

Bella didn't break her gaze from mine. Which told me I was going to need to answer. I sighed and offered her a weak smile. "He took me on a date." That was good, right?

"You have to kiss boys if they take you on a date?"

Nope. Not the lesson I wanted to teach my daughter. "No, no," I said as I raised my hand. "You kiss a boy if you like him, not because he gives you something." I could see this going sideways fast.

Bella's lips parted and formed an *o* shape. Then she wrinkled her forehead. "So you like Mr. Holt?"

My stomach dropped at her question. I realized that I had walked into that one, but for some reason, I hadn't prepared myself for how I would feel when my daughter asked me that question. It was something I'd avoided asking myself all week. "I did."

I wanted to avoid giving that answer, but I didn't want to lie. I was tired of trying to pretend that I was okay, and Bella looked so intrigued that I decided to be honest with her.

"You did? You don't anymore?" she asked. She rose up onto her knees and placed her hands on either side of my face. She concentrated her gaze on me, looking deep into my eyes.

"I still do," I whispered. I feared she would be able to see my lie if I said anything different.

Bella held my gaze for a moment before she nodded

and flipped to sit down on the bed again. "I like him," she said as she pulled the comforter up over her lap and patted her legs.

I blinked a few times as I watched her return her attention to the TV screen. She liked Danny? Had I miscalculated this? "You like Mr. Holt?"

Bella nodded. "Yeah. He's funny. Well, when he's not sad." She glanced over at me. "He's been sad lately."

My heart squeezed at her words. I wanted to believe that he'd been sad because of me, but I didn't want to get my hopes up. "Oh?" I responded.

There was another question I wanted to ask, but I wasn't sure how.

"He should come over more. I like him."

My body froze, and all I could do was blink and process what she'd said. I glanced over to see her smiling up at me. "You want me to invite Mr. Holt over for dinner?"

Bella nodded. "Yeah. And you can kiss him too."

My cheeks flushed as the memory of his lips pressed to mine washed over me. It was strange to get permission from my daughter, but also kind of reassuring. Even if Danny and I didn't work out—if he decided that I was truly too much work—it was good to know that I could find someone else. That I didn't need to be single forever just to protect my children.

And then my gaze landed on the brown envelope on my dresser drawer that held my past and also the key to my future.

My divorce papers.

I was ready. I was ready to sign those babies and return them to my lawyer. I was ready to be done with that marriage, and I looked forward to what was coming next. I wanted that to be Danny, but I was preparing myself for the fact that my future with him was probably non-existent.

I pulled off my covers and padded over to my dresser. I grabbed the envelope and opened it. After locating a pen, I began to sign. I flipped through every page and fervently scribbled my name. With each page—with each signature —I felt better and better. I was lighter. I was calmer.

I was ready for my future, whatever that held.

I took a deep breath when I was finished, shoved the papers into the envelope, and set it back on top of the dresser. I would drop these by my lawyer on Monday.

Instead of crawling back into bed with Bella, I decided to get ready for the day. After a long, hot shower, I dressed and did my hair. Then I put on some makeup and headed out to the kitchen. Tag was sitting at the table, eating a bowl of cereal.

After his weekend with his dad, he'd come back in a better mood. He was kinder to me and more willing to help out. He even smiled at me, which was a pleasant change. I wasn't sure if it was because he had Craig back in his life, or because he missed me while he was away, but I wasn't going to question the change.

I was just going to enjoy it.

I started the coffee machine, and just as I moved to

lean against the counter, there was a knock on the door. I furrowed my brow as I crossed the living room and pulled open the front door.

"Victoria?"

Victoria was standing in front of me. Her hair was pulled up into a bun, and she looked more relaxed than I'd seen her in ages. She was even wearing a white sweater and jeans—not her normal business suit. "Hey, Shari," she said as she pushed past me and into the house.

"Please come in," I responded as I moved out of her way. She may look happier, but she was still the same pushy person I knew.

"Thanks," she said as she turned around and ran her gaze over me. "Is that what you are wearing?"

I glanced down at my comfy clothes. "Yeah. It's Sunday morning. What am I supposed to wear?"

Victoria clicked her tongue. "Not that. Go change." She waved toward my room.

"Why would I change?"

Victoria's expression soured, and I could feel her frustration. Then she took a deep breath and offered me a smile. It was interesting to watch Victoria work through her emotions in real time.

"We're having a book club meeting. So go change."

I knew she was lying, but the fact that she was trying so hard intrigued me. So I sighed and made my way toward my room. She must really care about whatever this was to go through all this trouble.

I settled on an ankle-length floral print dress and my

jean jacket. When I got back out to the living room, Victoria was still there, looking impatient. When she saw me, she perked up. "Ready?"

"Yeah. Let me get my kids' shoes on first."

She shook her head as she placed a folded-up piece of paper into my hand. "I'll watch them. You just go."

I gave her a skeptical look, but she just shook her head and pushed me toward the door. "They'll be fine. I'll be fine. Just go."

I hesitated, but when she kept pushing me toward the door, I hurried to grab my purse and I headed out. After all, wherever she wanted me to go had to be better than standing here with her staring me down.

After climbing into my car, I punched the address into my GPS and headed down the road. I was headed to the beach, but for what was still a mystery to me. I pulled into the parking lot once my phone announced, "You are here," and pulled my keys from the ignition. I slipped them into my purse and got out.

I scanned the beach, and when my gaze landed on a man's tall frame, my entire body froze. It was Danny. Standing next to a picnic blanket covered in all sorts of food. He was staring out at the ocean, and he was dressed in a suit and tie.

My heart started galloping. I wanted to run away. I wanted to run toward him. I wanted to dissolve on the spot. I feared what he had to say, and I also feared what would happen to me if I turned away.

Danny must have sensed my stare, because he turned

and his gaze met mine. He stared at me for a moment before he offered me a small smile and extended his arms. Tears filled my eyes as I dropped my gaze to the ground. I didn't deserve this. I'd thrown him out of my life. Why was he being so nice to me?

The sound of gravel crunching drew my attention. And a moment later, Danny's shoes appeared in front of me. I tensed as I felt his body lean in to me. I wanted to lean in to him as well. I wanted to wrap my arms around him. I wanted to hold on and never let go.

But I'd hurt him. Did he even want me back?

"You came," he whispered, finally breaking the silence that surrounded us.

I nodded, but kept my focus on the ground. We didn't speak, but Danny also didn't leave. He remained in front of me. The weight of what we wanted to say surrounding us.

All of my pain, all of my happiness came to a head as I parted my lips and said the one thing I'd wanted to say ever since I pushed Danny from my life a week ago.

"I'm sorry."

When Danny didn't respond right away, I brought my gaze up to see what he thought. His eyebrows were knit together, and he was staring at me. Hard.

"I am too."

I frowned. What did he have to be sorry about? "Why?"

He scrubbed his face with his hand. "For pushing you. I should have let you take your time. I..." He brought his gaze back to me and squinted for a moment. "I want to be with you, and I'm willing to do whatever it takes."

This was music to my ears. I couldn't fight the smile that emerged. And when I saw the relieved expression that passed over Danny's face, I knew things were going to get better. I was going to be happy. Not only because I was discovering who Shari was, but because I was moving forward.

"I want that too," I whispered.

Danny moved closer to me but hesitated.

I didn't want him to worry about how I was going to react. Plus, he deserved to see me take steps toward him like he'd done toward me.

So I closed the gap. I wrapped my arms around his neck and pulled his lips down to meet mine. Instantly, his hands met my waist, and he pulled me in close. He crushed his lips down on mine. It took my breath away as we stood there, kissing like our lives depended on it.

My wall around my heart broke down, and all that was left was me. A woman wanting to love a man. And he wanted to love me back. How did I get this lucky?

When we finally came up for air, Danny leaned forward and rested his forehead on mine. He had a drunk happy smile on his face, which I was sure mimicked mine.

"Are you ready to try again?" he whispered.

I nodded and rose up onto my tiptoes to kiss him once more. "Yes."

He pulled me into a hug, and I wrapped my arms

around his shoulders as he buried his face into the hollow of my neck.

Even though my future was still a mystery, I knew one thing. I was strong. I was capable. And I deeply and wholly liked Danny. This was the start of a new Shari, and I was ready.

Bring it on.

————

Victoria

Bella was staring at me as we sat at the table. She was eating cereal and hadn't broken her gaze from me since I sat down in front of her. I tried to offer her a smile, but she just kept shoveling Fruity Pebbles into her mouth.

Great.

"Are those good?"

She narrowed her eyes.

Well, that didn't work. Maybe it was a good thing that I'd dropped out of the mayoral election. After all, if I couldn't win over Shari's kid, how did I expect to win over an entire town?

My heart ached at the thought of what I'd given up, but I wasn't going to dwell on that. Not after I'd made my choice. I was going to focus on my future and not my past. I was going to rewrite Victoria's story, and it started now.

Sure, I didn't know what I was going to do when it was time for me to clean out my office and walk away from the job that I thought I'd wanted my whole life, but that was all right.

For the first time in my entire life, my future was no longer planned out.

And as frightening as it was for me to admit that, I also knew that I was going to be okay.

I was finally free, and that was all that mattered.

Everything else was just a matter of details.

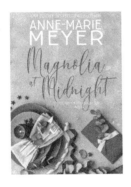

I have so many walls built up around my heart, and I'm not sure I have the strength to break them down.

I hope you enjoyed A Magnolia Friendship. I loved diving into Victoria's story and giving Shari her new lease on life. I wanted to show the growth of her confidence and ability to understand what she has always deserved.

The next book in the Red Stiletto Book Club series is **Magnolia at Midnight**. In the next story, Victoria discovers who she is now that she is not the mayor of Magnolia. Plus, I dive into Fiona and her story!

Grab you copy HERE!

Want more Red Stiletto Bookclub Romances?? Head on over and grab you next read HERE.
For a full reading order of Anne-Marie's books, you can find them HERE.
Or scan below:

Made in the USA
Middletown, DE
12 August 2024

59031276R00156